for

for...

> the People have asked me, "Why?"
> and i have responded, "Well, listen…"
> Yet the People do not listen.

2.

Later that day…hours have passed.

I find myself at the impersonal drugstore, picking up my prescriptions. The fluorescent lights make the situation bland, and i pay for my pharmaceuticals with indifferent anticipation. i exit the store, cross the trashed dirty lot to my car, get in and drive away. I know that – ah, suburbia…driving liquidates mental cohesion s

ometimes, and the mind runs rampant. Heading home, in the neighborhood, the trees stand in militaristic position – much like the Conspirators –, their branches saluting all those who pass, piss, past and present. In the passenger seat sit my pills, in a plastic bag, and crickets, in a small brown paper bag like a lunch bag. i have lizards as pets. Why?

i look to the right, as i often do when i drive, sensing a presence that is not actual. Oftentimes, i open my mouth to speak, but no one is there to receive my words, and I am forced to ingest myself myself. This Time there is the movement of the insects and the personality of the pills. i turn my head back and focus on the road. A succession of three manhole covers litters the gray paved street like mines on a battlefield of a war of complacency. i swerve to avoid tire contact with the rusted discs, pleasingly indulging my compulsion to do so. Shortly thereafter, and the sirens wail in my ear. Here we go again:

The policeman is classic: white, sturdily built but starting to gain weight with age. I assume that he was once in the armed forces.

"Do you know why I pulled you over?"

I think to myself, He speaks the Language slowly, retardedly, disjointedly, forcibly dignified. Trying hard...

All of a sudden, it seems like he's been speaking for hours. And about what I have no idea, for his words have led me into some type of mental paralysis. Is he a master of vocal tonal hypnosis? No matter how hard I try to pay attention, i can't follow his talk. I'm trying. i'm trying. He is winning... i focus on his mannerisms, on his face. i can't keep my eyes off his block head, and I find myself staring at this cube head on this cube neck on this angular body for quite some Time. It blows my mind, for Ii have never before seen such rudimentary laws of geometry thusly applied to the human skull.

Evidently, however, the Officer of the Law is growing intensely insecure, and suspiciously demands that i get out of my car. He has found the goofballs,

but i have the right papers.

"i am in Exile," i inform him. i look around at the trees that grow out of the ground alongside the street in front of the houses. There is my car and his car. The sun is going down. i look at him as he flips through my papers.

Then he grumphs, nods, and steps back – curiously, cautiously, not sure whether he can take his eyes off me. He walks back to his car; i smile, thoroughly pleased,

relieved, like i had to pee for hours and then finally peed, and i get back into my car, and drive on home, safely to safety.

the TICKING of the RESIST.

You see, i wear a watch for I must keep schedule.

      But Ii cannot tolerate the ticking of the Seconds Hand, so forcefully dull and causally so casually reminding me of the omnipresent Time, of which I need no reminding.
      Sitting at my desk, typing away... Stopping to think, the tick, tick, tick, tick, tick, tick, tick as if it tick tick tick as if it tick tick can't think STOP! Unlatch the clasp and jettison Time! Ii need no more of You, but You refuse to relent. You have failed your own purpose, for now I know not what Time it is is is is is is is is

        is is is
        is is is
        is is is
        is is is
        ======
      is is is is is is
     is is is is is is is is
   is is is is is is is is is is
   is is is is is is is is is is
   is is is is is is is is is is
     is is is is is is is is
      is is is is is is
        ======
        is is is
        is is is
        is is is
        is is is
        is is is
        is is is
        is is is
        STOP.

i look over at where my watch has landed. My fury has somewhat abated. But I see myself walking across the room, picking it up (know face glass cracked), biting into it, chewing it, gnawing on it,

>and finally swallowing it…digesting its parts…then shitting it out, flushing it down the toilet, washing my hands, and returning back to my desk.

But decide not to.
i am alone in this room.
i am alone in this room.
i am in this room, alone.
i rise to my feet and feed my lizards, then feed myself a drink. i sit down at my desk in my brown study, drink my drink and drink another and watch the bearded dragon snap the stupid crickets into its mouth. i drink and then remember my pills and so i search for them and i find them and then i swallow very many of them.

Who needs the barren wastelands? I wonder.
The burrowing owl sustains life on the prairie grasslands. Its natural habitat is being rapidly destroyed, or so asserts my calendar. Few of the People seem to care, however. Why should they? Why should the People concern themselves with the fate of the burrowing owl, a creature with little to no direct relation to anything in any of the People's specific microcosmic dwellings inside the great Nation? Who knows if these animals even exist?

If Ii am unlucky, and I know that i am prone to bad luck, the People may like me someday. My fortune has been that that someday is not today. Yet I can look ahead and be optimistic, and comfortably believe that this will never be. My misery, even then, would be posthumous, and in heaven or hell or the truth of the silent pasture of the Nothingness, the matter would not matter. Why should it?

And so i sit again, uninspired. i used to write only when i
was inspired. But Time has changed – well, not really. Still,
either way or even so, I am no longer left with a Choice. i don't
even have a Chance.
    And so it is my personal, inert duty to do what i must do.

IV.

My psychiatrist told me that i was crazy. I think that psychiatrists
shouldn't say such things to their patients. She told me that i was
impatient, too. It is possible that i misheard her or that I
misunderstood her.
    She has given me many pills, for which Ii am very
grateful. i utilize them in addition to the others that I have
prescribed myself.
    She has told me many things, few of which I accept, most
of which i refuse to believe. Ii have suspicions that she is among
the Conspirators – perhaps even an Elite Conspirator (though I
kinda doubt it) – and though she may be good at heart, she could
be, potentially, as evil as the rest. Therefore, there is no way that i
can trust her. i don't trust her. I don't trust her at all. However, I
see my assignment to her and my Time with her as an opportunity
to learn. How much does she know?

    I do not blame her, though, nor do I blame them. I
comprehend their hatred of me and my ways, at least from their
perspective. When one considers the roots of their philosophy,
and the fact that i attempted (and hopelessly failed) to raze the
very foundations of their empire, their treatment of me is perfectly
understandable. And if this is my punishment, Ii have no choice
but to welcome it with open arms.

    In retrospect, it was a foolish thing to attempt – WAR,
opposed by such a massive, obedient, and nationalistic army.
Now my mind is my prison and their continuance my torture.

FIVE.

There were a few smart Ones-to-be in the entire Force...I will tell you...

About one year ago, a group of three Elite Conspirators of the Magisterial Order (Queen + two Bishops [with two knights {of the sub-Magisterial, or simply Conspirator, Order}], to be exact) appeared before me as i walked down a Neutral Street in Noland, where nothing real ever really happens.[1] Noland, this bland land that Ii live blive e e be in, hates me and so i must hate or (do?Ii) love it,

:*fact*: The five of them appeared before me, not really there, yet present nonetheless. They lacked spirit, but possessed bodies. I had read about Encounters, and had seen them on the television and in the movies. Due to my non-compliant nature, I had always expected the day to arrive – and here, at last, it was (and here, at last, they were).

::::::::::::::::::::

One woman and four men, all non-
descript and painfully alike...dressed
in uniforms of bright yellow and white.
The road was deserted.
The confrontation was for us alone.

They stood in an obviously pre-discussed sentry-like position. i smiled at them. Maybe i was a bit nervous. I wasn't, though. Maybe i was arrogant.

but here it is...

---

[1] and what was i doing there in the first place, I wonder? no, I know... they have their ways...

Bishop **Queen** Bishop
Cavalier   Cavalier

Bishops flanked Queen. The men alongside the Bishops took two steps forward and one step in, towards each other, aligning themselves in front of their respective masters.

    "Hello!" i greeted the fools with a facetious warmth that took them a bit by surprise. Queen lifted her arm, elbow bent at a prominent ninety degrees, palm facing me.
    "I will not stop," i told them, still smiling. She closed her fingers over her palm *signal* and the two Cavaliers swarmed (if two can swarm) around me in an oft-practiced (simulated virtual reality training) gambit
                 [as a soft breeze blew the leaves of the trees that lined the street]
            ; they grabbed me tightly by my upper arms
jelly
felt;
i did not motion to resist.

-Queen Conspirator approached me with syringe in hand.
-Bishops presided over ceremony in prescribed dignified silence.
-Queen rolled up my left sleeve; the tight grip of the Cavaliers served as a tourniquet, and the Queen herself (! an honor, ? !) slid the needle into my protruding mainline. She pushed the stopper in.

    "You have already done this to yourself," she informed me, holding a now empty syringe. The poison had begun to take effect even before they had injected it, and Ii did not give a shit about their world. A Bishop then stepped forward and presented me with a vial that evidently contained the antidote...but I knew it to be only more venom of lies and deceit.

"Here, Bastard…" Bishop.2 spoke, "this is your One Last Chance."

Queen nodded, the two horses released me, she uttered, "Neither turn a deaf eye nor a blind ear, for we know you know the Truth."

i as i and I, i took my One Last Chance into my hands, grasping the alleged counter-agent in my fist, naturally steady with narcotic confidence.

Staring at the red liquid as it percolated gently inside its glass vial, it occurred to me that i was already dying – that this "Cure" was a dreadful elixir – a ruse! – , more malignant than my already present disease. At that moment, I realized that they were trying to contaminate me by dosing me with their cursed bile, leaving me alive and hell, doomed to subsist as a baneful worm in their falsely florid existences. so

i opened my hand and let go of the vial, watching my One Last Chance fall to the ground, watching the glass shatter against the concrete. tiny pieces of broke-
glass scattered slightly upon the street amidst the red liquid that bubbled truculently and ate away at the cement a good four inches deep.

"You are finished, Bastard," Bishop.2 informed me. i stared at his face and saw nothing in it. "We were instructed to give you One Last Chance," He continued, "which you have clearly failed to accept. The Magistrates will be duly upset with your poor decision." He paused, and i waited for Him to conclude his curious speech.

i smelled in his voice that he had spent much Time memorizing this mesmerizing slew of lines, and concluded that He must be of the lesser intelligent of the Bishops. This disappointed me. i had learned to have much more fear of the silent Ones. And I thought that the Magistrates would have had more respect for me. Then again maybe they thought it safer to send a less thoughtful believer. Makes sense. He continued: "You are now then sentenced to Exile. You are from hereon confined to live with yourself, by yourself, excepting the provisional legal contact allowance with your anointed appointed Godperson. You will maintain your residence, and you will die when we are ready to kill you."

Presently, the silent Bishop (Bishop.1 – the one of the two Ones) stepped forth and handed me a manila envelope. So dearly did Ii desire to ask all of them how they could take themselves seriously. Their bright colored armor was obnoxious and blinding.

i grabbed the envelope and turned away.

"Tell the Magistrates that I am pleased," i yelled to the Conspirators without turning around. i knew they were no longer there, but I knew that they could hear me.

SIX.

I had known for quite some Time that an Encounter was inevitable. Encounters, few and far between, are reserved for certain of the People. Because the People can not be individuals. They must all remain the People.

An order for an Encounter comes directly from the Magistrates. Encounters are the institutionalized control mechanism against dissidents, implemented in emergency situations in order to maintain general order. Encounters mean one of two things: death or Exile – usually death...
:and are mandated to quarantine the nonconformists, to silence by revocation of human contact – .

Death is death. It's quite simple how that works. To explain Exile: a one of the People thusly sentenced thereafter legally deals with no others of the People, having been strictly and systematically and programmatically and bureaucratically cut the fuck off from interpersonal contact – excepting, of course, the provisional Godperson, who functions as a monitor...who functions as the eyes of the Magistrates, or at least as the eyes of the Elite Conspirators of the Magisterial Order. What she sees, they see. For if you are still alive, you must be watched.

The Godperson serves this purpose.

6.

Exile has turned out to be a blessing – one of the highest points of my (low)life. I know that i am expected nNothing. and i have been granted Time to think. I enjoy to think.

but i have been granted Time to think.

?why?

The People are destined to overcome; this Truth has been planted in the far recesses of their minds accordingly, and the People instinctively, unconsciously, know this to be true. But of course it is *not* True, it is merely the subliminal pacifying mechanism that allows the perpetuity of the Clock.

See this now, and listen; I will play it for you:

the Magistrates – the most powerful entity, the Ones who designed the Clock and control Time and rule the Nation –, they are the Ones who preside over the Elite Conspirators of the Magisterial Order, who in turn preside over the Conspirators, a designation which includes three branches: the Hismen, the Officials Elite of the Good Men, and the Solid Folk. All units of the Clock preside over the People, by will of the Magistrates according to the Mandates of the Magistrates.

The Magistrates, through the auxiliary branches, allot the People certain privileges as incentives for obedience, though they know as well as I do that these incentives are wholly unnecessary.

The People will follow anyway. The reason that the allotment of privileges is theoretically needed lies in the fact that the People will overcome something – not Nothing. And, in overcoming something, Nothing will never change. The Magistrates have a deep understanding of the world.

And I understand their desire to manipulate the People – it's just that I choose to remain isolated from their world and their organizations. It is thereby that i rejected my acceptance into the Force with the following letter:

It is with the best of intentions, to all parties concerned, that i decline my acceptance into the Force. In the simplest of terms, i wish not to take advantage of the People - not for my benefit, nor yours, nor theirs.

My intelligence has become a blessing to me, and a curse to you. It can be no other way. Rest assured that you have my utmost respect, as I comprehend well your projects. i kindly ask you not to concern yourselves with me, a self-declared fool, for i will only prove detrimental to your worthy cause.

i will not apologize for my decision, for I am not sorry. i humbly ask you to please regard me as the tiniest of specks of dirt that will in no way interfere with the cogs and the spokes and the chains of the well-oiled wheels of the machine that is the Clock.

If this letter reaches the right hands, I trust that i will be understood. Good luck to you in the future.

Sincerely,

your Bastard
151-75-3507

I supposed that the letter fell into the right hands, that it reached the right people – and that the Magistrates realized that i posed no threat to the Clock. After all, I thought, if I ever feel the need to make a change, i'd never be able to find enough followers!

I thought Ii knew this to be true: that, because of the letter, the Magistrates would know that i want as little to do with their world as possible; and that, newly compelled to remain withdrawn from their world (as a duty to their system as well as my own, in admittance of my defeat and their triumph), I no longer find it sensible to incite any more fruitless disturbances that only promise to attract more attention upon myself. Such was my rationale.

This was after the War, of course, and before the Encounter. It was after the War that they asked me to join the Force. And it was after my declination that they issued the Encounter.

So, evidently, I was wrong.

In the same light, if you are reading this or any of my other writings, it means that i am most certainly dead. Whereas I wish to be a catalyst of chaos and change (and am aware of self-contradiction), my sensibilities remind me of revolution's sole function in theory and prevent me from wasting my Time pursuing such idealistic endeavors.

SCENES FROM THE era of beneficent non-Truths (the era of errors): A HISTORY LESSON (Part I)

In my day, i have observed little change. The few changes that have been made were made to ensure that Everything stays the same (meaning: the Clock stays on Time!). The folly: Everything today is headed in a downward trajectory, thus making No Change a guarantee that things will continue to head for the worse. This is, however, my opinion.

Obedience and service and subservience are unconscious and involuntary – the People do not oppose because they are satisfied.

For example, good literature is hard to find. Most libraries have been shut down, and those that persist to this day contain no more than maybe a thousand or so harmless books. Though the People are responsible for this, the Hismen must be given credit for their brilliant execution of the Free Will Epidemic in the early fifties. The FWE is a self-perpetuating virus (released by Mandate of the Magistrates) that gives the People a Choice, and the obligation (*freedom*) to express their Choice by their ways of life. This is, however – and I am risking belaboring the point here – merely a ruse.

In other words, the Hismen have never had to censor books, – because nobody wants to read them. Revolutions never need to be repressed because the People don't want to revolt. Illegal drug trafficking is nonexistent – this is the duty of the Officials Elite of the Good Men, and I might add that they do an exemplary job. Concomitantly, the crime rate is at a stable low, because the People have the ability to procure anything they want through nominally hard work. Criminals do exist, but they work for the good of the Nation and are employed by the Hismen – by Mandate of the Magistrates, of course – just like anyone else.

However, it is important to note that anyone who fails to function properly is an illegal criminal (an admittedly curious distinction) who must be punished. Therefore, let it be understood that a bus driver who fails to show up for work is as illegally criminal as a man who kills his wife without being mandated to do so. And there are, of course, institutions and rehabilitations for the People who commit illegal crimes.

      "That's very interesting, but I asked you why you think you were sent here to see me..."
      "i'm getting to that – you just need to *listen...*"
      "Okay...but first let me try to understand: you think you're an illegal criminal, then? That's why you've been punished, why you're made to come see me every third day?"
      "Oh! Like you don't know!" Really! "Allow me to continue to explain to you that which Ii believe you already know..."

      The Magistrates have studied societies in great depth, from this place to that place, this time to that time (insert impressive knowledge of history here). They have analyzed and interpreted the specific qualities of each part of every society and have evaluated each societal quality's importance in relation to the overall order of the ideal Clock. Therefore, the Magistrates understand the relevance of criminals, their impact on past systems and the ideal system, and comprehend that their role is an essential component to a functioning and well-rounded society. ?So why not ascribe criminality to certain of the People and control it (and arguably, by sanctioning legal crimes and legal criminals, do away with criminality altogether)? The criminal's job is as crucial as that of a baker's or a farmer's or a cashier's, a doctor's or a teacher's or a carpenter's or an engineer's – the People work together in perfect unison in calculated measurements. The People's duty is to themselves and to the Nation, and not one of the People's roles is more important than another's – the tasks may be more numerically demanding, more qualitatively difficult, more quantitatively requiring – but all needs are singularly equal for the ideal system. That is why there are more television repairmen than publishing houses, more cashiers than artists, more women than men, and more toilet seat manufacturers than postal workers = equals = a highly calculated equation for maximum efficacy of every of all of the People for the prolonged sustainability of the Clock.

Speaking of postal workers, I truly believe that the Communications Breakdown of 2057 was just as deliberate as the West Fire of 5024 and quite possibly even the B Dispersion of the late thirties. (I will attempt to refrain from using any further dates, because of their inherent meaninglessness. Our calendar has been altered so frequently that dates bear little significance. The mentioning of the three previous dates is made only because the events are synonymous with them, though any attempt at chronologically situating them would be impossible. Within the next few decades, the calendar will undoubtedly be changed a few more times, and the Communications Breakdown will have occurred in -35, 1500091, 2046, or any other such arbitrary number – even though it will still be called the Communications Breakdown of 2057. Past dates are immaterial and knowledge of them does not benefit the People in any way.)

The Communications Breakdown of 2057: Technology, electronic communications and computers, began wiping out the classic forms of communication and social practices – most significantly postal mail and the use of the telephone. The post office and telephone companies began losing relevance, power, and money. These stocks were failing (as others rose, of course), but too many businesses were going bankrupt, and too many of the People were losing their jobs. Automation of communication became problematic. Concurrently, the People were intaking so much useless information at a humanly intolerable rate that their minds became overloaded and virtually fried. Their attention spans reduced drastically, their ability to focus on their given roles became more and more compromised. The situation grew so severe that over half the population of the Nation was virtually brain-dead and no longer capable of functioning on their prescribed levels of personal work and Clock function.

The Magistrates had avoided action until it became evident that the entire population of the Nation was about to succumb to this cancer of the mind, at which point they mobilized the Hismen. Had the Magistrates waited one or two weeks longer, all the People might have been rendered completely incapacitated. It was absolutely necessary, for the subsistence of the Nation under the order of the Clock, that the Hismen release the trans-mutated neurological E-coli virus via the Neuro-Center (NC). The NC, located in Capital Borough in the Norlandish Region, is the birthplace and/or tollbooth of all Public Access Data (PAD). Any and all information the People are allowed is either created in the NC or passes through it for inspection. The NC transmits all of its information to millions of stations throughout the Nation via the Data Transmission Wires (DTW), which transmit the information to homes and businesses.[2]

So, to make a long story short, ninety percent (90%) of computers Nationwide failed (as planned). The majority of the People were capable of involuntarily and instinctively recommencing their normal lives and routine practices (as was hoped). The post office and telephone companies were back in business (good work). And most of the laid-off workers got their jobs back (well done). Order was restored.

On a side note, the already low unemployment rates decreased even more, as the Hismen had created new, less powerful, less threatening computers which demanded a work force to be manufactured and implemented. Unfortunately, the post office never fully regained its popularity. And as far as concerns the People who were irreparably retarded by the Communications Breakdown of 2057, they were either found jobs on par with their newly inferior mental ability, or they were renovated or eradicated. The People are, after all, expendable.

---

[2] The Magistrates, it is said, comically refer to the data transmission wires of the NC as "Rectum Wires," no doubt because they serve as a means of shitting on the People.

VIII.

i sleep
ten hours a day and still have trouble staying awake. Each day is
followed by another as the preceding.

i went out again today, to get more goofballs. They
actually have pharmaceutical dispensers now, much like soda
machines. First you slide your card in, to confirm access to
permitted narcotics. As i am in Exile, the Magistrates realize that
my sole function is to serve as proof of an idea, and whatever i do
cannot truly be detrimental to the cause. More simply: i have
access to any and all narcotics I desire.
Drugs are necessary and must be valued. The Magistrates
know that addictions
motivate the People
and can give them a purpose in life.

Standing at the vending machine earlier today, i scanned
my card, and as the tiny screen on the upper right flashed
"ACCESS GRANTED," some simpleton brushed against me. His
exhalation of breath invaded my nostrils tasting thick, musty,
disgusting, as his shoulder gashed into my upper back and scent
chill tremors down my spine. i shuddered violently at the fool's
touch disgusting disgusting. And – ! – he *kept on walking – as if
nothing had happened!* – until he disappeared from my sight.
"you dumb shit," i murmured – his shoulder press still
imprinted on below my neck, violating me with his senseless
psychological squalor. "…you pusillanimous, vile automaton …"
and
so
then
i
felt   and

furiously i punched random numbers into the machine without
reason. Bottles and bottles of pills fell down into the collection
bin like a waterfall of HATE and

like a feverish junky
possessed by the
prescience of an
imminent sickness,

i grabbed my
pharmaceuticals
and ran out
of the drugstore.

CHAPTER NINE: TACTILE IMPRESSIONS.

"Fuck i still feel that ugly man's shoulder pressing against me like
a mountain, the lingering presence of his filth some crazy
unstoppable glacial mental water torture, pushing and pushing and
pounding and pounding and pounding and pounding…"
    "Okay."
    "What?"
    "Okay," she says. "I understand – "
    i let out a laugh, a little more vicious than I had intended.
"You don't understand; you're programmed to say that and to
write it down and imbed it in your patients' minds so they feel
they're not alone – but let me tell you something: I am alone. i
am in Exile, and that is a fact. and Ii see their eyes in yours."
    (My Godperson, so maliciously and sardonically appointed
me by the ever so clever Good Men, is a psychiatrist.)
    "First, I'd like you to tell me why you found this man's
touch so offensive…so repulsive."
    "My sensations are mine. I wish them to be mine alone, I
wish to govern them myself, and for them to not be impaired by
the thoughtlessness of simple-minded ignoramuses."
    "But it is impossible to live your life sensing only those
things that you choose – without sensing anything that's beyond

your control. You must admit that when you inhale through your nose, at any given time during the day, you may be smelling something that you wish you weren't."

"That is why i hold my breath when sweaty men cross my path and inhale hedonistically when a beautiful, well-perfumed lady walks past me."

She laughs with the noticeable color of condescension. I can't hold it against her. I think for a moment, then speak again.

"I don't expect you to understand everything i say. i'm not here because i *want* to talk to you. i ask you to try to understand *that*. i am here because i am in Exile, a sentence that was decided upon by the Magistrates up on high, who sent the

Conspirators to Encounter me. this has nothing to do with you – understand *that*."

"Could you please explain once more what you mean by the words you use...like 'exile', 'magistrates', 'conspirators'?"

"You – " i break, trying to calm myself. "You play along very well if you are among them. If you are not among them, then you serve (very well but) only as an optical transmitter. And, in my eyes, only further prove their existence."

"Proof?" she inquires, weakly affecting sincerity through a thin veil of forced concern and pensiveness. "Am I the only proof of this?"

"What, are you shitting me?" i can't help but blurting out. (There's only so much self-control I can exert.) "Ii need proof? Look around you. i see them every day, and so do you, and so does everyone else in this blind, stinking shit-hole of a Nation. They look like anyone else, but they are the Ones."

"What ones? What do you mean when you say, 'the ones'?"

I feel like i'm teaching an incubatory fetus here, giving a lesson to this poor woman, and I hear the desperation seizing my nerves. i close my eyes, focus on breathing: inhaling, exhaling, inhaling, exhaling. i relax ever so slightly, and decide it best for me to take advantage of the few opportunities i have to exercise speech. "The Ones – the Magistrates...the Elite Conspirators of the Magisterial Order…the Conspirators…the Hismen…the Officials Elite of the Good Men…the Solid Folk…"

"And who are these people?"

"No, they are not the People. Be careful with the words you use. The People are the masses. The People are not the Ones, the Ones are not the People. They are above the People…"

"Okay…what roles do the Ones serve?"

"Good…roles. This is the key to understanding the Clock." i look her in the eyes, she returns my gaze. i continue.

"The Ones is a generic term for all of the governing bodies within the Clock. The leaders of the Ones are the Magistrates. They basically run this whole fucking show." She looks up from her notepad, attentive, pen poised. It occurs to me that she doesn't need a fucking notepad – not only because she probably is solely a surveillance device, the probation officer, of the Magistrates, but furthermore because the Magistrates already know all this shit. This is unnecessary information for them. I then decide that Ii should enjoy wasting their Time, showing off what I know. The absurdity of this thought gives me great pleasure, and i smile.

"Beneath the Magistrates are the Elite Conspirators of the Magisterial Order, the Ones who directly preside over the Conspirators. The Conspirators, as a whole, include the Solid Folk, the Hismen, and the Officials Elite of the Good Men – there are no regular Good Men, I don't know why they have the privilege of being distinguished as Elite." I immediately consider that parenthetical aside as potentially being a subconscious jab at the Good Men. Then I think, and then i say, "But that might be because the Good Men are decidedly the most reliable of the three branches in terms of maintaining the ideal of the Magistrates' vision of the Clock. They are *constantly* utilized.

"The Officials Elite of the Good Men are essentially enablers and suppliers. They make sure that the People get what they need – in order to be able to perform their functions and maintain their roles within the Clock with the utmost competency and without complication. The Good Men generally operate within the model of the [(function)/(work/personality/family status/race)] –based exchange, wherein the People are given what they need on the basis of who they are (curiously enough, personal chemistry in terms of personality traits are remarkably left alone by Magisterial Mandate of the Clock). Although the Good Men, under the umbrage of the Magistrates, can totally refurbish personalities, they rarely exercise this power; quite humanistically – ha! – and unnecessarily, they refrain from such direct and blatant manipulation of the People. So, personality being the only variable, it must be kept in check (indirectly). Understand?" She nods, but I'm not convinced.

I don't know if i understand, to be perfectly honest. i go on anyway. There's little difference between talking to her, talking to myself, and writing. After all, what the fuck do I care if she understands? What the fuck do I care if you understand? i don't know her. i don't know you. You don't exist. Understand?

"The Good Men ensure that there are adequate religious institutions and educational systems – be they...whatever... The Magistrates, like i said before, don't like directly controlling the Peoples' personalities through specific reconfigurative alterations at the individual level – because that would admit that they acknowledge individuality amongst the People, which they don't want to. And they don't have to. All they have to do is control the world that the People live in, and everything that shapes their growth, their maturation, their ideas that the People think are their own. They make sure that the jobs the People "need" are there for them. The jobs and the churches and the voodoo dolls, the money, the education, the drugs, the prophylactics, the hospitals, the prisons, the indoor bazaars (aka superspaces), the vacation packages, the insurance – even others of the People like doctors and teachers and businessmen and pilots and cashiers – all of this is taken into account in order to steer the Nation in the right direction. The Good Men are the Ones who are responsible for this indisputably monumental task.

"The Hismen execute the Immediate Mandates of the Magistrates, which are issued only when complications arise and disruptions occur that destabilize the Clock as patrolled by the Good Men. The Hismen are well-trained and highly intelligent – they have to be – but they are, ultimately, utterly subordinate. If something unexpected happens, like the Communications Breakdown and all the shit that it caused, the Magistrates call in the reserves. They instruct the Hismen on how to handle the situation (the Magistrates have a thoroughly deliberated prescribed solution for nearly any given situation [though they obviously did not for the occasion of the Communications Breakdown, but that's not the point]) and the Hismen carry out the Immediate Mandate. That is their function, and they serve it well.

"Then there's the Solid Folk – or celebrities, as I'm sure you refer to them. They are the only of the Ones whose individual persons are made public. In fact, that is their function – *to be public*. Their lives are prepared for public viewing, awareness, spectacle, scrutiny. They exist to be liked or disapproved of, to be positive role models or bad examples…pipedreams or media happenings, businessmen or con-men…politicians or heroes…

"the Magistrates, like i said, are the highest lords and judges of this system – they rule their apparitors and all of the Nation…even Noland, which they hold is truly Neutral…even on a Neutral Street. The Magistrates are responsible for the Clock, which they designed and implemented I have no idea how long ago. Nothing happens that doesn't come down from the Magistrates. They are in total control… they created and structured and safeguard the world that we live in."

i take a deep breath, and look at the woman. My mouth is dry.

"Did you just write all of that down?"

"Most of it…" She looks up and smiles. "It's, I find it very interesting…and the Hismen, – why are they necessary?"

i sigh, more exhausted than disdainful. "Simply put, they restore order. (didn't i just go over this? where the fuck was her pen then?) They are the wide-reaching tentacles of the Magistrates; if something falls from the hands of the Good Men, the Hismen are there to catch it. it's because the Magistrates asked the Hismen to implement it. you know…………………: earthquakes…computer viruses…wars, assassinations…long lines at the stamp machine…stamps…"

i jerk my head up and try to keep it in place, still.

"…the Magistrates…began this world as we know it…and it is their intention…to continue ruling over it… They started the Clock…they created the Nation…they wrote the existence and the experience of all of the People within, including – but by no means especially – you and me."

My chest feels heavy and i'm short of breath. It seems more difficult than it usually is to breathe.

"Have you ever seen, or met, or had any contact with these people – I'm sorry, any of the Ones?"

i lift my eyebrows with my eyes closed. My head begins to sway to the left, i put it back up and it starts to fall to the left again. i try to get straight,

"What? i'm here, right?... i wouldn't be here otherwise… The Conspirators confronted me…, i experienced an Encounter…I knew it was coming,, too…they came to me, you see…by Mandate of the Magistrates… and the Good Men, you know,, selected You, as my Legal Godperson…I know…, the Solid Folk just as well as, You do –, they're in the magazines…,, each day, and on the television… and the Hismen…" i pause to swallow. my mouth is like beach paper. "no," i continue slowly, "i've never seen a Hismen… and…none of the People have ever seen the Magistrates…,, though they've contacted me several times…"

"Why did they choose to contact you?"

My whole body is swaying. i take my hands from my lap and place them on the armrest of this big comfy chair that seems to be trying to swallow me whole. Will you eat me, chair? Ingest me. Rid me. Rid the Clock of my Time. Ii have no Time. I want none of the Time, I want nothing of the Clock. I want it end over now.

i look up at her with some difficulty. i finally respond:

"Choose…" i stretch the word out downscaled, then repeat the word…stretch it out in high to higher pitched glissando… "Choose?" Then

"Ha! i didn't win the fucking lottery here, doctor. i am in Exile right now – does that mean anything to You?"

                                        She looks at
                                        my head, i see,
                                        with such vapid confusion;
                        I   realize that
              speaking with her   will   get

            me
         nowhere.
i feel ill.

"Enough,"

                                                        i say,

                                                "I've had
                                        enough," i throw a
                                                lethargic
                                                waveforapath
                                                eticemphasis.

i need to remember that I cannot reasonably expect her to believe

me, or expect anyone to believe me…the People have lived this

way all their lives – Ii come along and tell them they are wrong –

how could and why would they believe me? Why should they?

Why should you? Why should i?

                                                        And,
as often happens, i've come across too hostile, too angry, too
anxious. I must control myself better. I want to. i will.

      i get up slowly, trying to direct my balance and my
strength and my body. i walk to the door, and right before i leave,
i turn around, and i tell her, and i say,

      "If i could draw you a garden,
      i would draw it here. In the garden
in the garden
      in the garden,
         everyone knows
      what happened in the garden...

      ...but that

      has nothing

      to do

      with this."

our eyes meet   ;
air direct contact.

i leave.

ThEN.

what does this mean
what. does. this. mean.
w.aht soed. .hsi.t .e.nam.
?

                                                                    ?

I feel like i was just here, like i've already told her everything
before. Wasn't i just here? ...I can't explain why i'm here again.
But i'm still here. Again i'm here. Still i'm here. Again. Still. I
try to think. how did I get here? where was i before? is this the
same day, the same time, the same week, the same year? maybe
this is a different place. you know Time... a new place, or a new
Time. there is no way I can find out. how can I be sure? and
how could I be sure i;m sure?

                 the Clock plays its games, I know. i also know, the
Clock plays its games. and

                                                              she
                                                              will
                                                              never
                                                              unders
                                                              tand
                                                              no
                                                              matter
                                                              how
                                                              long i
                                                              sit
                                                              here
                                                              and
                                                              try to
                                                              explai
                                                              n it.

They
will
never
unders
tand,
and it
is
made
to be
this
way –
the
Magis
trates
have
organi
zed
everyt
hing
so
secure
ly, so
beauti
fully:
all is
well
and all
is
good
and no
one
cares
becau
se no
one
knows
.

Shit;
i have to get the hell out of here.
i must.
I thought i just did.
          but i'm still here.

                              what the fuck

          "You're the only person with whom i am allowed contact.
i live in solitude and i am allowed one visit to you every three
days."
          "Why?"
          "Why? Ah, what the fuck, …because it's best this way,
because the Magistrates studied and did their research and they
found that this is the way for the People and this is the way for the
Nation and this is the way for the Clock. The hands of the Clock.
Well oiled machine. Well. Machine. Clock. Makes sense," i
stand up and look around, this place like a room, all brown of
shades different with a little yellow and green
here   and   there.
They know this, too; the colors mean s o m e t h I n g – not so
much symbolically as historically and presently most beneficent
to this woman and to her specific patients, to the architect and to
the builders, to the painters and to the toilet bowl manufacturers.
All is well but   my head is about to explode,
showering shit brain feces urine nervous sociopathic aneurysms
on the brown shag carpet, boiling and bubbling and then to be lost
in the two-inch-thick-shit-colored-carpet.
gaseous
                    my stomach hurts and it's tight constricted and
gaseous
          hurts   tight
     stomach   and   constricted   gaseous
my   it's   and
                                             and my
                              head   god my
                              head.

        i step across the floor, feel my feet depression carpet
walking alone difficult tight-rope balancing act squish of shoes
nearly audible, make door, tight hold grab knob gotta get out gotta
get out twist knob and pull towards open. "i have to go now," i
exhale. I feel her look, her eyes behind her prescription-less
glasses unknowing and indifferent. No longer at all confused,
because she understands it all the way she needs to understand it.
She's content.

what does this mean?
head want some shit.

Ten.

My doctor suggested that i should go out. So the other night, i
went out. i went to a bar.

        i walked in.

        He pours me a scotch and soda without asking. Evidently,
i have been here before. He seems to remember me. Maybe i
have been here before…maybe i haven't. I decide not to worry

about it. i take the drink in my hand and drink it down. It tastes
good, feels good. He pours me another. i wait a beat, so as not to
seem anxious. i take a sip. Then take it all. Shit, it feels good. A
bit warm. He knows i don't take ice, just a splash of soda. Have I
been here before? I grow more curious, but i grow less anxious
with each drink.
        Hours pass. i've spoken with no one. i nod to the
bartender. He pours drinks. i like it here. The voices in my head
entertain me. My voice in my head entertains me. It's good to get
out sometimes, right? But I am careful not to interact with the

People too closely. I know what may happen if i break the Mandate of Exile.

The bar is brown. The surface is somewhat shiny. My glass is empty. There are many bottles behind the counter. My glass is full. I think about these many bottles, i read the labels and think about how each bottle tastes and how much a drink of each costs. i look at myself in the mirror ahead of me. i look at me. It is. Shall I tell you what i see? Would that tell you anything?

i look away. i look down. My glass is empty. Then it is full. i pick it up and take a drink, and think to myself, What am i killing here?

Myself, I answer, knowingly.

i look to my left. at the door. a woman walks in, not beautiful, but looks good enough to talk to. i hope that she sits beside me. she sits beside me. i hope that she comes home with me.

i look ahead again at me in the mirror. i shift my eyes slightly to the left to look at her in the mirror. our eyes meet in the mirror. i see that she is tired. she is weary. barman looks at me. fills my drink again.

looks at her.

“What’ll it be?”

“I’ll start with a beer.”

i see the barman’s reflection grab a glass, watch it pull a pint from the tap and place it on the bar in front of her. I notice

that my head feels a little heavy. It rolls a bit to the side and then i set it on straight.

i keep looking at her. i enjoy looking at her. Yes, her hair is red; it is longish, wavy, a bit crazy. But for her age, she has beautiful skin, slightly weathered, rougher than a late-thirties non-smoker. But she does smoke. And she drinks. i immediately ask myself, I wonder if she reads books. Ii almost fall in love.

Where is she right now? I miss her.

But instead, she is here at this bar now. I think about her. i itch to speak with her, i want to get closer to her, i want to brush up against her, to hold her, i want to touch her, to comfort her, to run my fingers through her hair.

i want to fuck her. i want to lay her on the floor, to take her and embrace her. i want to come with her.

i want to stroke her cheek with the back of my hand. i want to trace her eyebrows. i want to feel my lips against hers.

i want her.

Where do these thoughts come from, I can't help but think... What does this make me in this world? Does this mean that the Love-Heart Mechanism does exist within me? Why can't I control these urges?

i inhale every time she speaks, every time she shifts in the barstool, every time she breathes, every time she asks for another drink.

i think of the way the air changed when she first entered the bar...

i was there before she entered the bar. i didn't want to be there when she left.

But i was.

Many hours passed between the two occasions, of her coming and her going.

During that time, i went to the bathroom at least five times. The bathrooms were filthy. There were dark rings around the water's edge where it beached the bowl. No paper towels, no soap in the dispenser. i took to drying my hands on my undershirt

and being thankful that i could hold in the shit i had to take.

ONZE.

Reflex Existence will be the downfall of humanity.

Throughout the existence of man it can be observed that the People have become more and more reliant on technology and mechanical production and less and less on themselves, on natural instinct and immediate environment. Humans no longer need their natural instincts. Humans are no longer animals.
We have incubators to raise our children; we do not hunt our prey, but let machines raise livestock that the Good Men have carefully tweaked with foreign genes.

The severity of this situation becomes more evident with each passing day. Ii look around and see clearly the People being farmed as mindless automatons – they are given specific interests and instructions: they pursue the interests by following the instructions.

The People today exist by default. Mechanical and institutional reliance have become the only way to survive.

Subsistence is not pleasure or Choice but obligation and National duty like the body of the Christ that the Good Men created. The People live to serve their given purposes for the Nation. In fact, the Good Men administer tests to each of the People (during the incubation period) to best assign to each of the People a most suitable position. But the point is this: existence is

reflexive, in the sense that the People function on their designated levels solely by repetition, entirely without thought.

The People are drones, and they exist by default.

What I have yet to discover is why this is so. To ejaculate: I know and understand the motives and methods of the Magistrates. But do they comprehend their own actions, as to what their acts will inevitably lead → the Perfect Harmonious Society…is this their desire? The People are not individuals but

components. Alone they are Nothing but together they are the
IDEAL ORGANIZATION OF PEOPLE serving the Magistrates,
serving the Nation, and serving themselves.

   But, of course, the Magistrates know. This is, after all, the
Clock. And the Clock runs on their Time.

   so: therefore: read:

   (?) The People are happy and the Magistrates are
   happy (?) and everything and everyone is happy
   because everything functions to the desired degree
   of functionality in relation to the desired outcome
   – the masses are tools – in pleasure to serve, to be
   used;   in
      pleasure of the Magistrates – to be served
                     and to use

                  ....

The People cannot think about their situation and question it,
because they were never taught how.

                              Keep them busy and all is
                  well.
the People need to be kept busy   for
if they are not kept busy,   if they are not kept busy,
they become idle and depressed.   they may think, and write.

12, XII, and TWELVE.

the Magistrates granted me my freedom and i was happy because i thought it meant i'd be free but i'm not and i won't be, and anyway we all rot underground either way and i can't say i'm happy anymore not to suggest that i ever was happy. sometimes optimism invades me for short periods of time, like a foreign virus incapable of surviving in its host body. it gets inside, pokes its head around, looks for sustenance, hungers, starves, dies.

      i think i could have learned more had i stayed with them. ah, listen: i have no regrets but those of a lost education, a missed opportunity to learn more. the reason i chose not to stay with the Force was because i could not tolerate those fools; it was wholly my Choice, and i know i did it for the best. i probably would have killed myself by now had i been constantly directly subjected to their absurdities.

      there is so much that i know; yet i feel as if i still do not see everything completely. i am missing something, yes, something crucial that should allow me to see more clearly –

what am i missing that prevents me from understanding wh-

y i was poisoned even though i posed no threat.

      because?
            they must control me nonetheless,
because *i am of the People.*

                     a sad truth,
                     The Truth,
                     The sad Truth,

because no matter how much i know, i will always be a part of it

all.   no amount of knowledge can suffice

to allow an individual to transcend its physical state. and so this is

my hell, my physical crate

.

what i have left?
is
i must uncover the mystery of their ways.
                                        nothing
                                        would go through all
                                        of this trouble
                                        without Reason

                        Reason

                reason

                         |
                         V

....
....>>>>>>>>>>>>>>>>>>>>>>>>>
<

                [it never ends: it keeps going]

THIRTEEN.

"Tell me something: I'm curious about your daily routine..."
"What?"
"Well, like, what do you do when you wake up in the morning? When do you wake up? What do you eat, what do you do, where do you go?"
Strange question. i don't know how to answer. i say the first thing that comes to mind: "no, i'm afraid that's unacceptable." she returns confusion.
"Well, how about this then: what did you do today before coming here?"
"Ah, i see! today i took the bus."
"And where did you go?"
"what do you mean? nowhere really i guess. i don't know. i don't – i got on the bus cause i thought i needed to take the bus to go somewhere, i don't remember where – in fact i didn't remember where.   maybe i didn't have to go anywhere, maybe i just needed to take the bus. i rode the bus around for a couple of hours. while i was on the bus, i tried to think about

whether i had a purpose for getting on the bus. but everywhere the bus stopped, i couldn't find a reason to get off. none of the stops were for me. this much was obvious. if i had had a plan, then it must have evaporated like desert water under the heat of the sun. after two and a half hours or so, the bus completed its circuit, and i recognized where i had gotten on. this made sense to me – this was for me. i could get off here, i thought. so i did. i went home. then i came here."

she asked me something about god, or God, I can't remember which, or what exactly she'd asked me. but what the hell, i said:

Religion functions as a motivational/release mechanism in the
Nation religion is like sports is like television is like drugs is like
vacation is like work is like sex is like reading is like crossword
puzzles and board games is like all the other pacifying occupying
exercises that the Magistrates have successfully implemented with
the help of all three Conspiratorial Branches to maintain order.
Keep them busy. And the hoax of spiritual attainment, the con of
the future benefits of purity and (near-)sinlessness are simply
brilliant, wonderful motivations.

Ten.B.

the image of the woman in the bar haunts me. i cannot explain my
being that night. she must not exist. why did she affect me so
much? what was the purpose of this scene? these sensations are
not mine. i simply cannot. it is a vile reaction that overcame me
that evening. these are those that must be quashed. i cannot allow
such losses of self-control, such losses of self. they render me
vulnerable, and vulnerability does not behoove one in battle. i
shall erase this aberration from my mind. she will no longer exist,
and i will not have to deal with understanding her role. this is one
of the only ways i have to fight against the force of the Ones.

XIV.

"So, you're a writer?" Her glasses disturb me. They are regular
glasses, black, normal, yet they bother me…intensely. i have a
sneaking suspicion that they are not real... what's up with this
woman? who is she?
 i remember she asked me something.
 "What's that?"
 "You're a writer, correct?"
 "Incorrect."

She looks confused, and I remember having mentioned my works to her at a previous Time. I cannot tell her the Truth. I try to explain, "What is a writer?"

"One who writes."

"Ah…by definition, yes, you are correct…i am one who writes. But *writers* can be of a horrible, twisted breed, who exploit a personal manipulation of words, words that were defined for *communication*. And then…they think it's *art*. And therefore they think it's great. And what the fuck is *art*?"

"A form of expression." Shit, she is quick with the book teachings. I think of the Good Men. I think of what institutions she's attended.

"Bullshit. Art is – art is bullshit. Art is lies and combat –"

"Combat?"

"With the inner self…" i lose my train of thought. For a moment i consider pouring my coffee out onto the floor. i don't know why this thought occurs to me. I decide not to, and take a drink from it instead. The scotch i poured in it hits me. Kicks me up a tad.

"Please don't interrupt me…okay…fuck…i can't remember what I was trying to remember to say." i rarely know what I am saying, ever, which is maybe why i enjoy writing…

"Originally, we were discussing you not being a writer."

This woman is driving me nuts. How is all this hard to grasp? Psychiatrists are supposed to fix the mentally deranged among the People, not to drive the only sane person in this land insane. Shit, *that it is right there*, is it not…if she is not One of them, then the Magistrates and the Good Men are utilizing her extraordinarily well. Either way, she is here to lead me astray, the evil temptress has presented herself to our tragic hero. Albatross! But Ii will stick along for the ride, because I am confident in my ways, and I know that they are the Ill. i must try to maintain, and not let her ignorance deteriorate my confidence.

Right, I tell her that i am a verbal communicator on paper, not a writer. A silent speaker, because no one will ever listen to me. And if someone hears me, they are incapable of understanding. Blind. One must see to read to hear. The eyes aren't listening.

"All my life, i have been misrepresented, misinterpreted, misheard, misinformed, and mystified. No One nor the People can touch me now, on my turf or on theirs. No person can tell me that i am wrong if i never say anything.
"Listen," i continue,
"List them," continue,
"Its stem," continue,
"system, the…" continue…

"What?"

"you see? you're not listening. stop looking and *listen*."

She asks me what my childhood was like. What kind of illness does she have? And my parents, as if i knew them? As if she does not know we are all incubated at birth and released, only into a larger, more metaphorical, incubator?…she will not bring me down…Ii have too much…too much to lose…

JYGYLDYK.17.

i had to go to the superspace today to fix my glasses. Couldn't see right. i had left them on the windowsill, and without realizing it, i closed the window down upon them. Luckily, i had purchased the two-year protection plan.

I told you i live in suburbia, right? Massive indoor spaces upset me. Unnerve me. Too many people, too much crap. Everywhere. And those fountains. God. A god. For these types of reasons, I often think about how i need to get out here. move somewhere. but where?

i park my car in the large open space next to the enclosed structure of the indoor bazaar. Walking down the extended interior hallway...my ears feel imbalanced. The lights that come down from the ceilings are long and white and bright and illuminate the long and white and bright hallways with buzzing rays that penetrate my skull and infest my mind with its hum-hum-hum lines of light, unfailingly inducing an intense anxiety in my person. focus...

i take my glasses to the woman at the eyeglasses store, where i had bought my frames less than two years ago. i explain to her my situation and give her my identification number. She sits down before a computer and invites me to sit opposite her. For the next several minutes, she says nothing, staring at the computer. i grow impatient. i become irritated. more.

How much longer must i sit here?
I wonder.

Has she forgotten about me?
Has she completely forgotten that i'm here?

What the hell is she doing, anyway?

What the hell am i doing, anyway?
Why am i here?

What the fuck?
Has she dozed off?
Have I dozed off?

Can't she say anything?
Tell me something?
Fucking hell!
What the fuck is the matter with her?

What the fuck is she doing at that computer? What is she
looking at?
After an eternal ten minutes, i can no longer control
myself:
"What the shit are you doing?" i blurt out. "i really want
to know. Seriously! i really want to know what the fuck you're
doing to that computer! Will you please talk to me? Look at me!
Say something!" Then I (oh no), (so) i laugh, taken aback and
admittedly amused at my own ridiculousness.
But she doesn't laugh, she is not amused. i quickly realize
my impropriety and apologize to her, explaining that i am hungover, that my mind operates unusually after a night of heavy
drinking – my circuits cross, don't know – and that i am really
sorry. It takes another six minutes to convince her to go back to
looking at the computer. Eight minutes later, she looks up and
says, "Your glasses will be ready three weeks from today." i sit
still as she proceeds to draw blood from my arm.

there, in that chair, i wait for to be able to see once again.
patient and silent and motionless, i pass their Time gazing at the
mirrored walls about me and following the hands that never cease
to trace halos for the Magistrates.

FIFTEEN.

i sit
here and this
place is
crowded with them. these
the People so old, the skin
                clings to the bones
                and sags down,
                                suspended

these are the People,
the old
the People,
and even they
do not have the Time.

17.

i love sleeping, but I hate the fact that i have to sleep. and i love
food, and i love to eat, but I hate the fact that i have to eat. at the
other end of the
rectum,
i love to shit, but I hate *having* to shit. and Ii hate having to wipe
my ass.
                it's these inescapable incontrovertibles, these
human facts, truths, needs, weaknesses, vulnerabilities, that
remind me of my unavoidable helplessness, my humanness. if i
did not eat or sleep, i would die. this annoys me.
        how do/will I feel about death? and the ultimate
        unanswerable, how will I feel when i'm dead?

                        i love life, I just hate having to live it.

18.

...the further in i hide,
the smaller the hole closes
in around me; the People and
the Ones, together, surround me. i
cannot turn around now, not without being enveloped in their ways. and i refuse
the only way away is away,,, to keep dig-
ging.... but the hole is too tight and my
mind is going to implode........all is
becoming a bit too enclosed and
narrow, i grow claustrophobic
in my space, and as i strive
for the light it only grows
dimmer.....................

XIX.

for the girls, I truly wish that i could smile. i try, but it hurts, and
my performance in such an attempt is no doubt implausible and
ends up getting lost. but it is for them that I wish i could cry.
likewise i try, but to no avail. my efforts are useless, and it leads
back to the idea that you can't change who you are. or

"you'll remember this
for the rest of your life"

i almost laugh
but I know that the output would not prove worth the input. who
is this to say that to me? and what would I get out of it? what do i
get out of anything? what does anything or anyone get out of me?
what is my purpose here? am i really so expendable? of all the
things that i need, that my body needs...who or what needs me?

CHAPTER TWENTY.

FOrty NINe. : 3 FACTS;(ThRee trUTHS):

1. just because a man is trying to kill himself, doesn't mean he wants to die.

2. "there are hands on my brain. they are not good hands. they are not massaging me. they are molesting my mind."

3. "ah, shit... i don't feel like i'm dying, i just feel like i should be, and i wish i was. dying can't be more painful than this, though it probably is, if i die this way. a drink will make me feel better, the ugliness hidden, the pain tolerable – i keep feeling better and better and yet always worse."

30.

what am i doing here….
what what what am i doing here
what what am i doing here…

      "i am going to die soon."
      "How do you know that?"
      "Why do you ask such stupid fucking questions you robot
you you know nothing you know not even Nothing."
      "What happened to your nose?" she's referring to the
scratches on the left side of the bridge of my nose where i often
experience an intense maddening itch last night i scratched it and i
scratched it and scratched it...too much…became...furiously until
the blood ran down my fac.e,,,;;.iii

30.

"It's been a while since you've been here." this is a fact. I see no
reason to respond. she looks at me. "How do you feel?" this is a
questionN.
i look at her. i open my mouth to try to speak. i fail. her eyes
look sad. she reaches with her hand to replace some hair behind
her ear. is this the first time that i've looked at her? tt can't be. tt
feels like it ss. is this the same woman? Ii no longer know.

      i begin speaking with her. I don't know what i say. i hear
a low buzzing sound around me. I can't make out what she is
saying, I can't make out what i am saying. bBut somehow we
converse

      then she says

"so you believe in predestination?"
why does she ask me this? maybe i said something about
it. I decide that i will answer.
"only insofar as we are all predestined to die. otherwise,
the idea of predestination means as little to me as a box of nails…i
have a house…i don't have a hammer...or any wood…"

the buzzing grows louder. the sound surrounds up from the
ground all around. and i don't understand through these clouds.

i am sick and i am dying.   Ii believe in the present:

a.s.l.o.w.a.n.d.p.a.i.n.f.u.l.d.e.a.t.h.l.i.k.e.n.a.i.l.s.i.n.m.y.h.e.a.d.n.a
.i.l.s.i.n.m.y.a.r.m.n.a.i.l.s.i.n.m.y.b.a.c.k.i.a.m.t.i.r.e.d.a.n.d.i.w.a.n
.t.o.s.l.e.e.p.t.o.l.a.y.m.e.d.o.w.n.t.o.s.l.e.e.p.t.o.l.a.y.m.e.d.o.w.n.t.
o.l.e.t.m.e.s.l.e.e.p.t.i.l.t.h.e.m.o.o.n.l.i.g.h.t.s.j.u.s.t.a.m.e.m.o.r.y.

My   My   My   My
back   head   stomach   chest
hurts.   hurts. hurts.   hurts. My head hurts. My stomach
hurts. My chest hurts.   My back hurts.

                rupture
        the heathens   inside me.   the pits of hell are
boiling.

                jump
        acid   s. the water's bad? i am already sick. you have
no idea.
        you have no idea.
                you have no idead.
                y   ou will have your ideal,
                wh n i will be dead,
nd ths will b soon,
my son,   i d d.

TWENTY and ONE.

"I wish i hadn't yelled at that poor woman at the superspace. that dumb fucking – I wish i had I wish i hadn't exploded on you, either or I wish i wouldn't you know? i don't want to have these regrets, feel this guilt. But sometimes I hate the things i say, and I hate myself for having said them, I hate myself in retrospect. I hate myself."

I decided to tell my Godperson about some of my dreams. Perhaps, more for her than for me – an apology, a treaty, a gift, a bone thrown. Catch, bitch!
i told her about the one i have often, the dream in which

there's a woman standing in front of a canvas, painting, working diligently, intensely focused on her work. she stands in the middle of a large open brown room the floors and walls made of wood, the windows opening onto clear blue skies, the walls stand high but i see no roof only blue. and i know that the room is raised on stilts like a lake/beach/water-house but there is no water below it's just raised like that in fact i don't know what's below i just know it's raised on wooden poles. she works and works and works, she has been working like this for hours if not days if not longer – but the canvas remains almost entirely blank. nearly all of her strokes do not come in contact with the canvas. she does not seem to notice, or at least she does not care. well...; i never see her face. the dream perspective is from every angle; i see the object from all sides and from above and from below, standard dreamscape vision...but i never see her face. her hair is like yours – longish, brown, down. but i never see her face, like i never see yours.

at the end of the dream she steps back and looks at the completed
piece – the canvas marked by only a few light strokes of paint.

     Dr. Psychiatrist, your opinion?
WRONG.
!.
?.

... .
"Do you mind if i smoke in here?"

"What?" she says; i seem to have moved her from some
stagnant reverie... "No you can't –... um, yes, go right ahead..."
     i pull out my pack and light a cigarette. i twist it around in
my mouth, the logo resting atop, facing up. for some reason i
always do this. a bad habit, I know.

     "What do you think this dream means?"
     "i don't know," i shrug. "it's just a dream. what do you
think it means? that interests me more. in fact, that's why i told
you about it."
     "Well, dreams can be very telling. They can be affected
by what's happened to you that day, what's on your mind, what
you're worried about, what you're trying not to worry about."
she offers no compelling explanation... then she asks
     "What else do you dream about?"

i often have day dreams of sorts, not so much dreams as visions
like apparitions illusions like ghost realities and i see
                                                                               i
remember...i've seen so many places, certain places i feel like I
know – places i've never been
to – I know i've never been
to
in real (meaning?) life.
But i can picture these places very
vividly, they come into my

mind – uninvited – and I associate specific feelings and actions
with each imaginary landscape. I know these places
better than most places i've actually been to. my visual grasp,
my cognition of them is superb, surreal, over real.
but where are these places? where do they come
from? do they exist anywhere else, outside
of my imagination? are they real? how real? is
there a level of reality I can grant them, some way to measure
their relative worth? sometimes I feel that these myster-
ious memories are
implanted in me in some disc like the pd=t disc but for dreams
instead of pain…or maybe they're spontaneous hallucinations…
Sometimes I am confronted with a difficulty in determining
which of my memories are real and which are imaginary.
but then
should this distinction matter?
does imaginary mean fake?
meaning that sometimes I am confronted with a difficulty in
determining which of my memories are real and which are fake?
        is fake in this context negatively configured?
        should it be?
        or should it be (could it be)
of greater value?
        I'm faced with the question of whether or not such a
distinction matters,
whether or not the imaginary versus the real is a valuable
distinction. what if i learn more from the inside than I do from the
outside?
            can Ii live in (t)here permanently?

how?

I decide to tell her about my recurring vision of my death.

My death…I see my death, and i feel my death.

I see myself walking down a street –
i'm in some big city, I think –
and i'm walking down the street,
but there are no cars, no people, no sounds at all.

a big city street, completely deserted, and the air stands still
between the buildings along the block.
I see myself from above, walking down the street, and then I see
someone approaching me, slowly but stealthily (a contradiction
made possible by dream-logic), and even though I see him and Ii
know he is coming to kill me i don't bother to turn around.

Because Ii am both the man on the street in the dream
and I am my dreaming self watching my dream-self,
i am the actor and I am the director,
i am the spectacle and I am the spectator,
so as I see the man approaching, i know that the man is
approaching.

and though I know what is about to happen to me i do not run or
hide or turn to confront him until the very last second –

when he comes upon me and then i spin around to face him to
look him in the eyes and at that immediate moment his arm
reaches around my body and slides the knife into my back tearing
into my flesh at the space between my right shoulder blade and
my spine and god i feel it it fucking hurts
and then at that very moment there is only I – and I can no longer
see except from above: my dream-self is gone, only my dreaming-
self remains.
so Ii never get to see his face or his eyes.

and it is this way that I see my death. I see myself on the ground,
face down, knife protruding. empty streets all around.

and I always feel the pain. And it really hurts; or, like, I expect it
to hurt when I see myself getting stabbed. But the pain is odd,
indescribable…like I feel the knife in my back…in my mind – I
actually do feel the knife – but it does not hurt like I think that it
would – it doesn't bleed, except in my mind. No, it does bleed.
The knife bleeds? The pain. Sharp and dull, not there yet present
nonetheless. Blackness in my eyes in my head. Flashes of dark,
brilliant pain. Do you understand brilliant flashes of black light?

Everything is gray. The air is gray. Except for the blood. The
blood is red. Of course. Red brown. On the gray. Blood
everywhere on the gray sidewalk. Blood everywhere. Ugly
scene.

again i see
that my words have thrown her into some trance, yet she begins
speaking an act. I know she does not care any more than the Ones
who have infected me. I know that i am dying, and this idea burns
inside of me, an innerwhelming gulf that surrounds my body
inside and floods my blood with the fire of the fear that
immediately precedes resignation. I feel like i am bleeding out
my mind and they have done it to me and they are the sole cause
of my suffering and all I can expect from them is
Nothing…Nothing but institutionalized false sympathy. They
cannot care, and I cannot expect them to care about someone as
low as i, in Exile, dying, breathing my last breaths and not caring
a single fuck about their system,

as they sit
and shit
and sit
in their shit
and sprout
within it,
as i sit,

wondering why i had left when they had kicked me out,
wondering why i was bruised where they had hit me,
wondering why i couldn't breathe when they were choking me,
wondering why i couldn't speak when they had silenced me,
wondering why i was dying when they had poisoned me.

But Ii owe it all to them. And Ii do not forgive them, Ii
need not forgive them, because they have done nothing wrong; or,
more accurately, they have done right by Nothing. The one lesson
that must be learned is that they are right. It is true: they are
right. Because if Ii was right, then everyone else would be in
accord with me, and the world would be a vastly different place.
Right? If the Magistrates are wrong – they are not wrong, they
cannot be wrong. They are not wrong, because if their ways are
wrong they would not be practicing them – they do what is right
and best, and Ii am wrong and worst. And some day, they will
stab me in the back. I know this because I have seen it hundreds
of Times and
someday, i will be walking down the city street, and a man
will be walking behind me,
following me,
at a much quicker pace,
behind me,
and at the last second
i will turn to face him
i will turn to face him on this street where the air is gray and
everything is gray but his brown trench coat and the blood that
comes out of my back when he stabs me with his silver knife but
the man grabs me as i'm already turning to face him because I see
him coming from above I see him walking towards me and
i turn to face him and he stabs me in the back with his silver pen
one sharp Time
and he leaves the blade inside my body and disappears,
leaving me in a pool of blood
on the sidewalk,
a body in the red on the gray.

and he turns the corner and disappears,
with unnecessary celerity –
unnecessary because no one is be there to pursue him.

TWENTY and TWO.

Right now, Ii can feel them hear them see them
                they
        are running around   me in circles,
some of them suddenly jumping back   or to the side,
but always maintaining

                        the circle formation

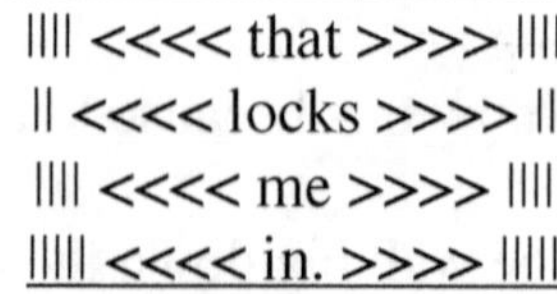

and as i look around me, as i look at this circle around me, I
realize that this circle
                is growing
tighter and
tighter
around me

        yet thicker and
thicker
beyond me
...   ...as these walls they...

                |||=>>>close in<<<=|||
                    \\\on///
                    \\\me///

.

TWENTY and THREE: My head is pounding and i want to cry

i want to

         scream

and i am back here trying to explain this again
(this chapter attempt of lucid break one last back to the irrelevant but i feel it is)
VII continuation of the Era of the Error it's the second part of the HISTORY LESSon:::

The greatest, and perhaps only, flaw of the Magistrates is their tendency to become overexcited with their discoveries and advancements – so much so that they sometimes overlook certain details in implementing them. After all – and this is important – they're only human. So, on occasion, they may fail to calculate with perfection the procedures and repercussions of every new movement. The Technology Age was a brilliant idea, but the People are not capable of enough self-control to allow free information to thrive.

      Another example is the aforementioned B Dispersion of ????. This is the only instance, that I am aware of at least, of alien life successfully infiltrating the Nation and corrupting the Clock. Well, maybe not the only instance – I do recall one other alien invasion, gratuitously named the Scare, – but that failed miserably, and it was easily kept hidden from most of the People. (Evidently, the alien life forms, incapable of breathing our air, died after two minutes and thirty four seconds. It was a thrilling UFO sighting that rapidly turned incredibly anti-climactic.)

      I was saying that the B Dispersion of ???? was an example of…example of what? The humanness of the Magistrates. They make mistakes. (Or do they?) There are two ways of viewing the incidence of the B Dispersion, in which aliens successfully assimilated into the Nation, appearing as of the People, resultantly fucking with the National population and unemployment rate. However, I do not have enough evidence to support either one of my theories sufficiently. Either way, I assume one of the following to be true:

1. The Magistrates, overwhelmed with glee by the sheer concept of the Employment Task Force Assurance (which assured every person of the People a job, recognizing unemployment as a job), failed to take into account grave deviations from projected population growth. So that when the Cresteds (the aliens) managed to infiltrate the NC so that the sudden millions of Cresteds materializing throughout the Nation appeared as regular, Nation-born citizens, the Employment Task Force Assurance could not compensate for this surprise population invasion. The Magistrates had no back-up plan for a situation this severe.

Or,

2. The Magistrates had pre-calculated the significance of unemployed citizens and their roles in functioning societies and declared their existences Vital (which they had), and decided that the Nation needed more. If this is true, then I propound that the B Dispersion of ???? was a hoax, or simple propaganda – a cover up that needed no covering up, involving some sort of concord between the Nation and the Crested Land.

I tend to put more credence in the latter; however, one must keep in mind that these are merely words that I have written down on paper – muddled, "paranoid" conjectures to which I have come in my endless hours of thinking. I make no claims to be presenting utter Truths herein; I feel not the need but the *desire* to document as much of the occurrences of this world at this Time, seeing as no one else is, in the infinitesimal hope that someone, in a future generation perhaps, following some drastic cataclysm, may find my writings, read them, and maybe learn something about the Era of Beneficent Non-Truths. In fact, I see myself as a present-day Herb Morrison of sorts, but the eye in the sky is now blind.

TWENTY and THREE: My head is pounding and i want to cry

i want to

scream

and my throat is dry as a desert, and there is no oasis except in my stomach. my body senses this, my stomach wants to come up to my throat. i jolt in my seat and cough, "Excuse me," and i run out her office door. i brace myself against the hallway wall, accidentally putting my hand against a glass frame of a picture which shatters under the sudden pressure of my palm. i look at the picture it's of a dog licking its paws it's a puppy a golden-haired puppy and its eyes are slightly watered from life and the trees lean up towards the sun the grass is tall and beside the dog is a single brown shoe with some water in it.

just the type of picture you'd expect to find in a place like this. i look at the pieces of glass embedded in my bleeding paw.

the bathroom is down the hall and i stumble towards it with a drunkard's conviction like a stabbed bull in the ring in the summer in the heat of the sun that glares down like an egg at the sand and the stands and the man and the beast, just making it but just not making it, and like that the beast lunges forward

and reaches the door and

i fall into it pushing it open and fall onto the bathroom floor vomit climbs up sideways out my throat and floors onto the floor in horrid expulsions of disease and waste my body is convulsing rebelling against me i grab onto the metal bottom of a

stall divider and clench onto it with a desperate futility sweating
heat the heat and the pain is the pain is biting inside me my head
claps inside my head violently swelling inside my cranium and
forcing out feeling cracking of my skull sharp
sharp pain i
grab my head with both hands
and
scream
shaking
vomit climbing out of my throat out my mouth and
                              scattering across
scattering across   the tiles
and sweat pouring out of my wanting body my stomach
shrieks sharp
head cries
as violent nightmares and my throat burn
burn together.
burn

23.

i cry and i scream and i cry, gasping grasping for air infrequently
involuntarily
because i want to die.

stop screaming.

i want to die.

i want to die.

die.

and TWENTY and 4OUR.

but they would not allow it.they could not see me die; no, not
yet.not when i would naturally have so much more of my life left
to live, so much more Time left to suffer.or at least, they could not
let me die on my own.it must be their doing, I kknow better.
          I know that the Ones are constantly growing in numbers,
in force, in control: their legs are stronger, their thighs thicker
with muscle, their stamina longer, - all of this all of this to
all to kick me and this kick me and kick me until blood flows
from my bruises from where they kick me.

they realize their strength, their invincibility, and my
fatality...

and in this bed i lie,
this bed of white
under these sheets of white
in this room of white.

in some building,
in this room,
in this place,
where i've been before
so many Time s

my mind harnessed,
alone with
my thoughts alone
i suffer, knowing
i can do Nothing
but wai t
in this blankness
in this whiteness

and
in here,
the monitors are visible
i am alone but for theire eyes.

i am
i am in the Core
and in here
they no longer hide
nor disguise
their methods
nor their intentions
nor their minions

one of them leans in to me
smell breath stank get away
whispers devilishly
"freedom is like a prime number"

that's not an original thought, fucker.
i read that fucking book, too.
"madness is like a prime number,"
i back away from the freak.

"there only exist the Ones and the selfs.
this is obvious to any madman, for
madness is always most obvious
to the madman himself.
therefore i know you pigeon."

CHAPTER.

for long Time and many days,

i have no way to know how long Time,
they
hold me here,
in the white,
in the Wait,
in the Core,
in the void.

they inject me with their
serums and cancers and diseases,
leaving me alone in a trance
to watch my mind dance,
as they operate on me and
study me, leaving me to spend
these days and nights unable to speak,
my mind and my thoughts my only
companion, and without paper
they torment me,
forced to tumble around
in my mind, to toss about
aimlessly, chaotically,
infecting, spreading,
eating away at what little remains of my stability, my. solidity, my
interior
my (all of my)
selfs
i have no Choice but to continue as i have

.

,

,
;
,
,
.

,
,

,   –   !

.   ,   .

–

;   .
,
.
.
,
,
.
,

(   )³

;   ;

;

;

.
____
³
,
,   .

"   ,"   .
"   ,   ?"
                ...   ...
            ...   .

"...   ,   !"

               ,   .
  .   -   '   /   ([,
 ]),   .

                          .

and 20 and FIVE.

I cannot go on. I see no reason.

     After they dispatched me from the Core, I returned to my home of peace and nothingness. A deep inhalation, a relieved exhalation. I sat on my couch and did not move for hours, maybe days, maybe weeks, maybe months, maybe years. I can no longer tell. Their intoxicants left me immobile, the way they want to keep me, I know. I must fight them to the best of my abilities, I must fight this terrible virus that they shot me with to the best of my abilities. I must.

     Yet I cannot possibly expect to overcome. Not when my opponents are so strong and I am so weak;
they have already made their move:
Check.
I can move my pieces, but the inevitable result will be checkmate.

We know this to be self-evident.

TWENTY and 6.

my organs ensure my torment, weigh my corpse, fill my lining,
full my form,
my body, *mon corps*, my core, my corpse,
my organs, my life, my systems, my innards, my inners,
my inescapable humanity.
I cannot deny my organs.
but I can deny my pain.
what I want is the body without a nervous system.
a body without pain.
that is the ideal that I seek.

TWENTY and SIX.

*"Do you remember when they changed the calendar two years
ago? No? Think about it. 740 days ago, it was 3033. Before that
it was 1968. Now it's 82. What do these numbers mean? 82 after
what? They are deliberately confusing the Time of the Nation –
and if they continue to successfully change the calendar every so
often, the Clock will never cease to tick. In defying Time, the
Clock will exist forever. How could it ever end, if nothing - not
even (and especially) its birth – could ever be temporally
situated? Things with no beginnings have no ends. This is their
goal. The Magistrates can rule infinitely by defying infinity by
controlling Time. Can't you see this?"*

TWENTY and VII.

what do they want from me?
        that is what I would like to know. I am here, I am here…is
that it? is that my function? where do I fit
in their puzzle? as some sort of passive reactionary how does that
benefit them how do I benefit them?
        KILL ME.
        stop looking at me. turn away – go. there are only so
many possibilities in Truth, and in the Truth, there only exist the
Ones and the selfs.

        I am here to rot like you, but alone.
        I am an extra, someone they had to Encounter I am runoff I
am waste I was lost in their message so they cast me aside kicked
me out of their home and I, disowned, am left here to kick it out
on my own because they fucked up because they forgot to add me
in and the sum is right or they added something by mistake and
the sum is too large so they subtract me the erroneous unit the
nonplussed surplus...

yet I serve them   ...... *because I have no Choice*   ......
but one of these days I will break free
but for now   I must wait –
exhausted,
extinguished,
my mind effete from constant useless meaningless contemplation
of what is;
                and oh – is, that i will never understand,
because i am not meant to understand,
and none of us
are meant
to understand

,that is all,

that,

and I am

I am

an error at birth

something

went wrong

during the

incubation process...

|

remembersomethingwentwrongduringthe pd=t disc installation
tthat must be it why | am in constant pain never properly set the
pd=t disc never properly set and/or

the

incubator was too hot or too cold maybe

| w a s

supplied with too much of one chemical and not enough of
another

| a m

imbalanced in a perfectly balanced society…

they must
know this yes | cannot be spared one faulty piece will ruin the
picture completely

| can be
cast aside but it will never work unless | am replaced with the
piece that fits but have they already found the piece that fits have
they already found that which can replace me have they already
found they are closing in on me yes because they know that
simply discarding me will not suffice

| must be
destroyed
terminate

erase
d

d

beca
use

use

                                        caca

caca

use
d

| exist as a symbol of their failure | am
the proof of their own humanness and
if they choose to get rid of me
they will be admitting
at least to me
their mistake
so they must
burn me in the inferno
and they must stab me in the back
as | walk down the street in the middle of a bright sunny day
and as | pass into the shadow of a building yes
the man will stab me in the back and disappear and

            the cleaning crew
                            | see them now
will come hours later to clean up my body
and my existence will leave no trace
except this

please
this please
this, please,
my final plea
for the Truth
the posing of questions to which I by nature constructed do not
deserve to know the answers

and to cease my mind I must stop my breath I am already
asphyxiated
I just wait
I wait hurriedly until they hold their grip one second too long and
then
            Nothing will matter for my matter will matter nothing
                    my questions will cease and I will not know
                                as now
but I will not ask
                    I will not wonder
                                            I will not think
                                                    I

                                                        will

                                        be
dead and my limp lifeless body will be
incinerated
            to leave   to leave
            to leave

                            n

                            o

                        trace

                        of the
        w   a   s   t   e   .

and XX and VIII. they came today to try to take my books
away
in the library
how humiliating
they can take my books from me but I will have them always as long as I
live different than their way I will not give in to their ways

the Ones are closing in
the Ones are closing in
(I hear the beating drums of the marching band begin)

while the world eats away at my mind

like a tapeworm through my psyche
burrowing like an owl

all that you see is all but that which you know **and
TWENTY and NINE.** I remember when I was young
I was locked out
of my house and I had to take a shit.
all of a sudden,
real bad.

I ran to my neighbor's house. I could hear them in there,
but they did not open the door. I ran back to my house, ran around
to the back, tried all the doors, all the windows. Stuck outside, in
between my home and the other homes, I couldn't hold it in any
more. I panicked, and I shit my pants.

It was a different home. Not the one I live in now. I was
very young then. My parents were still alive.

XXIX.

| received a letter in the mail, accusing me of numerous offenses,
slandering my name and falsely portraying various incidents.
More policemen. The Inspectors came to my house and insulted
me. The Magistrates have mandated a court date that | must
attend. | do not understand this demand in the least – if they want
to get rid of me, then | invite them to kill me as | see; if not,
LEAVE ME the fuck ALONE… Unless they want to keep me
captive, confined in their criminal or mental institutions… From
which | decidedly must attempt to protect myself…|'ve spent
enough Time in those places, mind you they do me no good they
do you no good | don't want none of that no more

THIRTY.

"So your hearing is coming up soon?" her eyes judge me crazy.
balls. |'ve seen these eyes before. balls! they come out of the
walls and land in the holes in the faces of the People so you can
look at me but you're not looking at me it's not you really because
your gaze is controlled by the Ones... But she awaits a response.
You will have your turn. but what has happened? nothing has
happened. | would have told you. so why is this happening to me
now?

    "Yes."

    "How do you feel about that?"

    Another brilliant fucking question. She's been nice
enough to me though, whoever the fuck she is. "They will do
what they will. | have suffered enough out here, | will simply
continue to suffer in there. Yet | do not understand why they pick
at me so."

    "What do you mean?"

"The Magistrates. I do not interfere with the Clock. I do Nothing right and also I do nothing wrong. I keep to myself, I believe that I keep up on my obligations and serve the Nation as an ordinary person in Exile which is my function my function being the best position for me in which capacity I can serve the Magistrates and serve the Clock most functionally and I believe that I adequately perform this duty. And as I have made it a point to stay out of their business, I think they could stay out of mine."

"But you've been charged with theft, trespassing, possession of narcotics, intent, assault, conspiracy, violation of court orders, numerous accounts of…-"

"WHAT? You believe that shit?" I still cannot believe how hopeless these the People are. I do not know what to say. I do not know where to begin. I already began!!! I began this a long Time ago! How can I – "The Magistrates used to treat me with respect, okay? They had to torture me, and I understood, I did not hold it against them because I knew that they needed to do it to keep order. But there is no order like chaos, and now they want me in prison. They already locked me up I never fought back I never complained I fulfilled my fucking I followed orders and now, as a reward for good behavior they are moving me to a smaller, darker cell, on the inside, in the inside. Without my books?"

she keeps talking
why does she keep talking
what is she is talking
STOP TALKING.
please stop talking

THIRTY and ONE.

I know nothing but the Nothing of the Truth that is what she cannot understand and I cannot understand why this burden must be upon me and what have I done what have I done for this where have I have I walked to where have I brought myself

"there is no reason for any of this to occur the Magistrates
have better things with which to waste their Time and should have
little desire to defecate any more of their shit on a People as low
as I but it will not end the Magistrates will not cease tormenting
me until I am dead
as an idea
I serve too little but as an idead I serve as an example – NO."

they would finally take me over YES
it is true
for I would become a bad example MADE PUBLIC → the lowest
and vilest of all the Solid Folk and in so being the Magistrates will
have ruined me completely
I have nothing left and more suffering and then death

or
death
come

now

XXX.

"I am a starving man, isolated, and a big plate of food rests on my
table. I suffer from hunger; I eat some of the food and feel ill. I do
not eat and I hunger. I eat more, feel sick, and vomit. I starve
from hunger and food makes me feel worse. I can starve myself
and die within a few days; or I can eat, and suffer illness until the
food runs out, and then die. NEVER I will not do this. You will
not take me down. For I know that I will be dead soon, so you
may as well kill me before it happens and take the credit for it.
YES. GRAB TAKE this is your opportunity and I grant it to you
and welcome you to my execution."

:

Come on in…

THIRTY and TWO.

in no defense my honor | wish not to
TAKE ADVANTAGE OF THE
                    employment task force
          intelligence is a blessing to me and a curse to
                    take into account grave deviations from for
myself or for anyone else   you have my reassurance
                                             the
Cresteds managed to infiltrate the NC
                         and
              | kindly ask you not to concern yourselves with
appearing throughout the Nation prove
detrimental to your worthy cause
                                             | will
              citizens the ETF plans
                              sorry if this letter
reaches the right hands
              "
The 'Hismen?'
"
                    HAVE NO BACK UP PLANS FOR YOU
IN THE FUTURE

                    and

       that is all your honor

                    ***

"so, in my defense, oh sir honor you,

"I wear a watch for I must keep schedule in
practiced gambit.
"they grabbed me but I
            "CANNOT TOLERATE
                "the ticking of the resist the third man
            approached me reminding
me of the omnipresent Time the tight grip of the men served as a
desk typing away stopping to think the tick tick tick protruding
mainline unlatch the clasp and jettison Time

                                                    'I
                        NEED,' I
                        NEED
                        yelled at the

                        man with the
                        ENTIVES
                        that are
                        wholly and
                        unnecessarily
                                            "

        empty

        you have failed your own purpose for now I
    even before they had injected it then presented me with
            a vial that evidently the sustains life on
                    DECEIT
            here bastard…this is your being
                            RAPIDLY DESTROYED
    few people to
            two men released me

        And I can only try so hard I can only push myself so far
and they still do not understand.

AN EPITAPH OF EPITHETS.

blow after blow, I open my mouth to speak and they hit me again.
My gums bleed and I open my mouth to howl in pain and again
the fist, knuckles to my face and I realize that it would be prudent
to keep my mouth shut to reduce injury. Better you than me, I
always said to myself.

      Deep inhalation, relief – exhalation. None of you know.
must stay calm now. Walk…

I just don't know anymore. I must think. Rethink.
What has happened here? let's start at the beginning...

When someone touches me, I am filled with this horrible sensation
of disgust and contempt. Shudder nasty giggle-likes repulsion,
convulsing. Contact is as a slug, slime, offensiv

last moments allowed to scribble drivel

This piece of writing is the piece of shit in my pants: the anxieties
– physically manifested – of the interior versus the exterior.

There is only so much your mind will not remember.
After that, you're screwed.
With forgotten dreams I sat idle, inundated in diluted,
futile obsessions; now I sit at peace, for this cell is a sanctuary and
speaks only truths. The walls are covered in scratches of pain,
and I must consider myself lucky, I guess, for I am still alive, if
that is lucky. And there are very few ways by which I can torment
myself in here. The darkness proves to shade my terms; the less I
can see the better.
I will have another three years and seven months before
they unleash me. I am unsure as to any of my previous
convictions or opinions – inside this cell there is nothing outside.
My fingers trace phrases of love and hate, fear and
restlessness…but I rest my palm in exhaustion over a cool
blankness. I lost the war I never wanted to fight.
There are no distractions inside. I still wonder whether or
not they will kill me, though it would not matter much anyway
anymore. There was so much I had driven inside myself, and now
I must purge. Tangibility is the Truth. Everything escapes my
vision but these bars, and I know that they exist and that I deserve
this punishment.

Three years and seven more months, my friend, and I will
tell you The Truth.

the garden.

NEW ROSES.

truth.

ONE.

       When someone touches me, i am filled with a horrible
sensation of disgust and contempt.   shudder nasty giggle-likes
repulsion, convulsing.   contact is as slug, slime, offensive,
immediately compelled to wash myself – though I know that no
water will ever cleanse my true filth, matter how hard scrub at
skin. feverish rancor boils in veins. bones composed yet we
break; what left all but   not. have squandered realities
exchange for returns nothing.   ?
 ask. listen.
 hear .
more can expect?
don't .

              twothree123,
              here are   unto Thee:

       fish swim steadily, through blue green, sifting shifting
shitting neverending struggle

...

        People asked, "Why?"
        responded, "Well, …"
        do .

2.

Later day…hours passed.

find   impersonal drugstore, picking up prescriptions. fluorescent lights make situation bland, pay pharmaceuticals indifferent anticipation. exit store, cross trashed dirty lot car, get   drive away.   – ah, suburbia…driving liquidates mental cohesion s

ometimes, mind runs rampant. Heading home, neighborhood, trees stand militaristic position – much like Conspirators –, their branches saluting those who pass, piss, past present. passenger seat sit pills, plastic bag, crickets, small brown paper lunch . lizards pets. ?

look right, often , sensing presence actual. Oftentimes, open mouth speak,   there receive words, forced ingest . This Time   movement insects personality . turn head back focus road. succession manhole covers litters gray paved street mines battlefield war complacency. swerve avoid tire rusted discs, pleasingly indulging compulsion so. Shortly thereafter, sirens wail ear. go again:

policeman classic: white, sturdily built starting gain weight age. assume he was once armed forces.

" you   pulled over?"

think , speaks Language slowly, retardedly, disjointedly, forcibly dignified. Trying ...

sudden, seems he's been speaking . about   idea,
his led into some type paralysis. master vocal tonal
hypnosis? try   attention, can't follow talk. I'm . i'm .
winning...mannerisms, face. keep eyes off block ,
staring cube   neck angular body quite . blows , Ii never
before seen such rudimentary laws geometry thusly applied
human skull.

Evidently, however, Officer Law growing intensely
insecure, suspiciously demands   out . has found goofballs,
papers.

" Exile," inform him. around   grow   ground
alongside front houses.   . sun going down.   flips .
Then grumphs, nods, steps − curiously, cautiously, sure
whether take . walks ; smile, thoroughly pleased,
relieved, had pee   finally peed,

,   ,

safely safety.

TICKING RESIST.

see, wear watch must schedule.
cannot tolerate   Seconds Hand, forcefully dull causally
casually reminding omnipresent , which need .
Sitting desk, typing ... Stopping , tick, , , , , , if
STOP! Unlatch clasp jettison !   , refuse relent. failed your
own purpose, now

======

======

.

where   landed. fury somewhat abated.   walking
across room,   (glass cracked), biting , chewing , gnawing ,

swallowing …digesting its parts…   , flushing
toilet, washing hands, returning   .

decide .
alone .

.

, .

rise feet feed ,   drink.   study,   another
bearded dragon snap stupid   .   remember   search them
swallow very many .

needs barren wastelands? wonder.
burrowing owl sustains life prairie grasslands. natural
habitat being rapidly destroyed, or asserts calendar. Few   seem
care, . should they?   concern themselves fate , creature
little direct relation anything any People's specific
microcosmic dwellings inside great Nation? knows these
animals even exist?

unlucky,   prone bad luck, may someday. fortune
today.   ahead be optimistic, comfortably believe   . misery,
, would posthumous, heaven hell   silent pasture
Nothingness,   .   ?

, uninspired. used write only   inspired.   changed – ,
really. Still, either way , longer   Choice.   Chance.
personal, inert duty   .

IV.

psychiatrist told   crazy.   psychiatrists shouldn't say things
patients. She   impatient, too.   possible   misheard her
misunderstood .

given ,   grateful. utilize addition   others
prescribed .

,   accept, most   . suspicions   among   – perhaps
an Elite Conspirator (kinda doubt) –   good heart, could ,
potentially, evil   rest. Therefore,   trust .   .   . ,
assignment   opportunity learn.   does ?

blame , ,   . comprehend hatred   ways, least from
perspective. considers roots   philosophy, fact   attempted (
hopelessly) raze foundations empire, treatment   perfectly
understandable.   punishment,   welcome   arms.

retrospect,   foolish thing attempt – , opposed by
massive, obedient, nationalistic army.   prison   continuance
torture.

FIVE.

were   smart Ones-to-be entire Force... tell …

year ago, group   Magisterial Order (Queen + Bishops
[knights { sub-, simply , }], exact) appeared   walked
Neutral Noland, real happens.[4] , land live blive e , hates
hate (?) love ,

                                        ::   , , nonetheless. lacked
spirit, possessed bodies. read Encounters,   television
movies. Due non-compliant nature, always expected   arrive –
, last, (, ,).

::::::::::::::::::::::

woman four men, non-descript
painfully alike…dressed uniforms
bright yellow .
deserted.
confrontation us .

stood   obviously pre-discussed sentry- . smiled .
Maybe   bit nervous. wasn't, .   arrogant.

...

Bishop
Cavalier

flanked .   took forward step , towards each other, aligning
respective masters.

"Hello!" greeted fools   facetious warmth   surprise.
lifted arm, elbow bent prominent ninety degrees, palm facing.

____

[4]   , ? , ...

" ," , smiling. closed fingers *signal* Cavaliers swarmed (swarm)   oft-practiced (simulated virtual reality training) gambit
[soft breeze blew leaves   lined]
; grabbed tightly   upper jelly
felt;
 did motion .

- approached syringe .
- presided ceremony   silence.
- rolled   sleeve; tight grip   served   tourniquet,   herself (! honor, ? !) slid needle   protruding mainline. pushed stopper .

" already done   yourself," informed, holding   empty . poison begun effect   injected ,   give shit world.   stepped presented vial contained antidote... knew   venom lies deceit.
", Bastard…" . spoke, "   ."
nodded,   horses released,   uttered, "Neither   deaf eye nor blind ,   ."
,   , grasping alleged counter-agent   fist, naturally steady narcotic confidence.
red liquid   percolated gently   ,
occurred   dying – "Cure" dreadful elixir – ruse! – ,
malignant than   disease. moment, realized   contaminate dosing cursed bile, leaving alive , doomed subsist baneful worm   falsely florid existences.
opened   let , watching   fall ,   shatter against concrete. tiny pieces broke-
 scattered slightly upon amidst   bubbled truculently ate cement   inches deep.
" finished, ," . . stared   saw . " instructed   ,"
continued, " clearly . Magistrates duly upset poor decision." paused, waited   conclude curious speech.
smelled voice   spent memorizing mesmerizing slew lines, concluded   lesser intelligent . disappointed. learned

fear . thought   respect .   *   safer send less thoughtful
believer. Makes sense. : " sentenced .   hereon confined   , ,
excepting provisional legal allowance anointed appointed
Godperson. maintain residence, die ready kill ."

Presently,   (.1 –   ) forth handed manila envelope.
dearly desire   seriously. colored armor obnoxious
blinding.

turned .
"   ," yelled   without turning .   ,   .

SIX.

known for   Encounter inevitable. , far between, reserved
certain . Because   individuals. remain .
comes directly .   institutionalized control mechanism
dissidents, implemented emergency situations   general . mean
: death – usually ...
: mandated quarantine nonconformists,   revocation – .
. It's simple works. explain :   legally deals   ,
having strictly systematically programmatically
bureaucratically cut fuck interpersonal– , course, , functions
monitor...   ,   . sees, .   , watched.
serves .

6.

blessing – highest points (low).   n.   granted . enjoy
.

.

??

.*.

.*.*.*.

destined overcome; planted recesses minds
accordingly, instinctively, unconsciously, . True, merely
subliminal pacifying allows perpetuity Clock.

, play :

— powerful entity,
designed rule —, preside , , designation includes :
Hismen, Officials Good Men, Solid Folk. units ,
according Mandates .
, auxiliary , allot privileges incentives obedience,
wholly unnecessary. anyway. reason allotment
theoretically needed something – Nothing. , overcoming ,
change. understanding .
understand manipulate , choose isolated
organizations. thereby rejected acceptance following letter:

*best intentions, parties concerned, decline .
simplest terms, wish advantage - benefit, yours,
theirs.*
*intelligence become , curse . . assured
utmost , projects. kindly yourselves , self-declared
fool, prove detrimental worthy cause.*
*apologize , sorry. humbly please regard tiniest
specks dirt interfere cogs spokes chains well-oiled
wheels machine .*
reaches , understood. future.

Sincerely,

151-75-3507

supposed , posed threat . After , , feel
able enough followers. — want , newly
withdrawn, system — admittance defeat triumph –,

sensible incite   causing fruitless disturbances attract .
rationale.

          , , .   join .   declination issued .
      , , wrong.

        same light,   reading   writings, means   certainly
dead. Whereas   catalyst chaos (aware self-contradiction),
sensibilities remind revolution's sole function theory prevent
wasting   pursuing idealistic endeavors.

**SCENES era beneficent non-Truths (errors): HISTORY
LESSON (Part I)**

 , observed . changes   made   ensure Everything stays
(meaning: !). folly: headed downward trajectory, thus
making   guarantee   continue   worse. , , opinion.
        service subservience unconscious involuntary –
oppose   satisfied.
        example, literature . libraries shut , persist
contain   thousand harmless books.   responsible ,   credit
brilliant execution Free Will Epidemic   early fifties. FWE
self-perpetuating virus (Mandate) gives , obligation
(*freedom*) express   . , – risking belaboring point – .
        ,   censor , – nobody wants . Revolutions
repressed   revolt. Illegal drug trafficking nonexistent –
, might add   exemplary job. Concomitantly, crime rate
stable ,   ability procure   nominally work. Criminals ,
employed   –   , – just anyone else.
        , important note fails properly criminal (admittedly
distinction) punished. ,   bus driver show   illegally man
kills wife   . , , institutions rehabilitations   commit crimes.

        "That's interesting,   sent ..."

" getting –   ..."
"Okay... first : you're , ? you've ,   come every
third ?"
"Oh!   !" ! "Allow   ..."

studied societies depth, place ,   (insert impressive
knowledge). analyzed interpreted qualities   society
evaluated societal quality's importance   overall   ideal . ,
relevance , impact systems   ,   role essential component
functioning well-rounded . ? ascribe criminality   (arguably,
sanctioning   ,   altogether)?   crucial   baker's farmer's
cashier's, doctor's teacher's carpenter's engineer's –
together perfect unison calculated measurements.   ,   roles
another's – tasks   numerically demanding, qualitatively
difficult, quantitatively requiring –   singularly equal   .
repairmen publishing , cashiers artists, women ,
manufacturers postal workers = equals = highly equation
maximum efficacy   prolonged sustainability .
, Communications Breakdown 2057   deliberate
West Fire 5024 possibly B Dispersion late thirties. (refrain
using further dates,   inherent meaninglessness. Our   altered
frequently bear significance. mentioning previous   events
synonymous ,   chronologically situating   impossible. Within
next decades,   undoubtedly   times,   -35, 1500091, 2046,
arbitrary number –   called . immaterial   .)
: Technology, electronic communications computers,
began wiping   forms communication social practices –
significantly mail use telephone. post office companies
losing , power, money. stocks failing (rose,),   businesses
bankrupt,   jobs. Automation became problematic.
Concurrently, intaking useless information humanly
intolerable   overloaded virtually fried. spans reduced
drastically,   compromised. grew severe half population
brain-dead capable   levels   .
avoided action until evident   succumb cancer ,
mobilized .   weeks ,   rendered completely incapacitated.

absolutely necessary, subsistence under , release trans-
mutated neurological E-coli via Neuro-Center (NC). , located
Capital Borough Norlandish Region, birthplace / tollbooth
Public Access Data (PAD).   allowed created   passes
inspection. transmits   millions stations throughout   Data
Transmission Wires (DTW), transmit   homes .[5]
        ,   long story short, percent (90%) Nationwide (
planned). majority   involuntarily recommencing normal
lives routine (hoped).   business ( ).   laid-off got   ( ).
restored.
        side ,   unemployment rates decreased ,   , ,
threatening demanded   manufactured . Unfortunately,   fully
regained popularity.   concerns   irreparably retarded   ,
par inferior ,   renovated eradicated.   , , expendable.

VIII.

                                                           sleep
ten   trouble staying awake.   followed   preceding.

        went ,   . actually pharmaceutical dispensers , soda
machines.   slide card , confirm access permitted narcotics.   ,
realize   serve proof , whatever   truly   . :   .
        Drugs   valued.   addictions
                                motivate

        .

        Standing vending earlier , scanned ,   screen   flashed
" ," simpleton brushed . exhalation breath invaded nostrils
tasting thick, musty, disgusting, shoulder gashed   chill

---

[5] comically   "Rectum Wires,"   .

tremors spine. shuddered violently touch. kept –
happened! – disappeared sight.
     " dumb ," murmured – press imprinted below ,
violating senseless psychological squalor. "… pusillanimous,
vile automaton …"
     Furiously, punched random numbers   . Bottles   fell
collection bin   waterfall

                          junky   prescience
                   imminent sickness,

ran

.

CHAPTER NINE: TACTILE IMPRESSIONS.

"   ugly 's pressing mountain, lingering   unstoppable
glacial , pushing pounding   …"
     " "
     "?"
     "," says. " – "
     laugh, vicious intended. " ; programmed
imbed   '   they're –   : . ,   .   ."
     (, maliciously sardonically   clever , .)
     ", I'd   man's … repulsive."
     " sensations mine.   , govern ,   impaired
thoughtlessness simple-minded ignoramuses."
     "   – beyond . admit inhale nose, during ,
smelling   weren't."
     " hold sweaty path hedonistically beautiful, -
perfumed lady ."

laughs   noticeable color condescension.   .   , .
"   .   .   .   , sentence decided   high,   .
– ."
          "   , , ?"
          " – " , calm . " along   .   , ( )   optical
transmitter. , ,   existence."
          "?" inquires, weakly affecting sincerity   thin veil
pensiveness. "   ?"
          ",   ?" help blurting . (There's   self-control   exert.) " ?
.   ,   ,   everyone   , stinking shit-hole .   ,   ."
          "?   , '?"

          teaching   incubatory fetus , giving   ,   desperation
seizing nerves. close ,   breathing: inhaling, exhaling, , . relax
,   opportunities   exercise . "– ...   ."
" ?"

          ",   . careful   .   masses.   ,   . above ..."
          "...   ?"
          ".... key ."   ,   gaze. .
          " generic term   governing . leaders   . basically
run fucking ." looks   notepad, attentive, pen poised. occurs
doesn't   –   probably solely surveillance device, probation , ,
furthermore   .   .   , showing   . absurdity pleasure,   .
          "Beneath   ,   . , , include , ,   –   regular ,
privilege distinguished ." consider parenthetical aside
subconscious jab   . ,   , "   decidedly   reliable maintaining
' vision . *constantly* utilized.
          "   essentially enablers suppliers.   –   perform
competency complication.   generally operate model
[()/(//family status/race)] –based .   basis   – , chemistry
traits remarkably   .   (umbrage)   refurbish
personalities, occasionally   . , humanistically – ha! –
unnecessarily,   blatant manipulation . ,   variable,   check
indirectly. ?" ,   convinced.
          ,   honest.   . difference talking , , writing.   ,
understands?   ?   .   . ?

"   adequate religious   educational – ...... , said ,
controlling Peoples'   reconfigurative alterations individual
level –   acknowledge individuality amongst ,   .   .
, shapes growth, maturation, ideas   .   """ .
churches voodoo dolls, , education, , prophylactics, hospitals,
prisons, indoor bazaars (aka superspaces), vacation packages,
insurance –   doctors teachers businessmen pilots –   taken
account   steer   direction.   indisputably monumental task.
     " execute Immediate   ,   complications arise
disruptions occur destabilize   patrolled .   well-trained   –
– , ultimately, utterly subordinate.   unexpected ,   caused,
call reserves. instruct   handle (deliberated solution
nearly [occasion ,   ]) carry . ,   .
     " – celebrities,   refer .   whose persons public. ,
– .   prepared viewing, awareness, spectacle, scrutiny.   liked
disapproved , positive models examples...pipedreams media
happenings, con-men...politicians heroes...
     ", , lords judges –   apparitors   ... , ...   ,
.   .   total ... structured safeguard   ."
          , .   dry.
     "   ?"
     " ..."   smiles. ",   ... , –   ?"
     sigh, exhausted disdainful. " , restore . (?   ?)
wide-reaching tentacles ;   falls   ,   .   implement .
...................: earthquakes...computer viruses...wars,
assassinations...   stamp ...stamps..."
          jerk   , .
     "... ...   ... intention... ruling ... started ... ...
wrote   , including –   especially – ."
               .   .
     " , met,   – ,   ?"
     lift eyebrows . begins sway , put   starts   .
straight,
     "? , ?... wouldn't otherwise...   confronted ...,
experienced ...   coming,, ... came , ...   , ,, selected ,

… …,   ,   –,   magazines…,, ,   …   …” pause .   beach .
“,” ,“i’ve   …   …none   …,, they’ve contacted several …”
        “   ?”

        swaying.   lap   armrest big comfy chair
whole.   eat, ? . Rid.   .   .   ,   .   end .
        difficulty.   respond:
    “…” stretch word downscaled, repeat …   higher
pitched glissando… “?”

            “ ! didn’t win   lottery , doctor.   –   ?”

                    vapid confusion.

        nowhere.
    ill.

“ ”
 ,

                                    ,

                        “I’ve ,”
                        throw lethargic
                        waveapath
                        eticemphasis.

    reasonably

,   … lived

    –   –

    ? ?

    ? ?

                                    , ,
hostile, angry, anxious.   better. . .

,   balance   strength . walk   door,   leave,   ,   , ,

   " draw   ,

         .

         ,

         ...

      ...

         ."

  meet.
air .

      .

. . . .
w.aht soed. .hsi.t .e.nam.
?

                                                      ?

      ,   .   ? ...   .   ?   ?   , , week, ?
different . ... , .   . ?   i;m ?

plays games, . also ,   .

                                                              ·   ,
                                                              –
                                                              organi
                                                              zed
                                                              secure
                                                              ly, :
                                                              cares

                                                              ·

     ,

          ·

       ·

          ·

           " person whom .   solitude   visit   ."
           "?"
             "? , ,... ,   research   .   .   ..
       ,"   ,   , shades
                                                                     ·   ,;
colors s o m e t h I n g –   symbolically historically   ,
architect   builders, painters   bowl .
explode, showering brain feces urine sociopathic aneurysms
shag carpet, boiling bubbling   lost -inch----.
gaseous   stomach hurts   constricted

                                    god
                              .   .

floor,   depression   tight-rope balancing act squish
shoes audible, ,   grab knob gotta   twist   pull . “   ,” exhale.
,   behind   prescription-less glasses unknowing .   confused,
. She’s content.

        ?

        .

    .

        suggested   .   night, .   bar.

            .

        pours scotch   asking. ,   .   .   … haven’t.   worry
.   . tastes , feels . . wait beat,   .   sip.   . , .
warm.   ice, splash .   ?   ,   .
        . spoken . nod   bartender.   drinks.   . voices
entertain.   entertains.   , ?   interact   closely.   happen
.

        . surface shiny.   .   counter.   full.   , labels
bottle   costs.   mirror . . . Shall   ?   ?
        .   .   .   . pick   , , killing ?
                        , answer, knowingly.

    .   .   , ,   . hope   sits beside. .   .
        . shift   .   .   tired. weary. barman .
fills .
        .
        “What’ll ?”
        “I’ll start beer.”
        barman’s reflection ,   pint tap   . notice
heavy. rolls   set .

looking .   . Yes, hair ; longish, wavy, . , ,
weathered, rougher - non-smoker. smoke. . ,   reads .
almost .

? miss .

instead,   . . itch ,   closer ,   brush , , ,
comfort ,   .
. lay ,   embrace .   .
stroke cheek   .   trace .   lips hers.
.

thoughts , ...   ?   Love-Heart Mechanism ?
urges?

, shifts barstool,   breathes, asks .
entered ...
.   .

.

occasions,   .
, bathroom . bathrooms filthy. dark rings water's
edge beached . towels, soap dispenser.   drying   undershirt
thankful   .

ONZE.

Reflex Existence   downfall humanity.
reliant mechanical production   , instinct
environment. Humans   instincts.   .
incubators raise children; hunt prey, livestock   carefully
tweaked foreign genes.
severity becomes   passing .   farmed mindless
automatons –   interests instructions: pursue   .

default.   institutional reliance   survive.

National   Christ   .   purposes . ,
administer tests   (incubation period) assign   suitable .   :
reflexive,   designated   repetition, entirely .
drones,   .
discover   . ejaculate: motives methods .
actions,   acts inevitably lead → Perfect Harmonious Society…
?   components.   ORGANIZATION   serving , , .
, ,   · , , ·   ·

: : :

(?)   happy   (?)   desired degree
functionality   outcome –   tools –   , ;
—

…………

question ,   taught .

busy   .

,
idle depressed.   ’   , .

12, XII, TWELVE.

meant i'd free   won't ,   rot underground
anymore suggest   . optimism invades periods ,   incapable
surviving   host . gets , pokes , sustenance, hungers, starves,
dies.

stayed . , :   regrets   , missed   .   chose stay
;   ,   .   killed   subjected absurdities.
              ;   . missing , ,   —

    prevents -

    poisoned   .
              ?   ,
        .

                                    sad ,

                                      ,

                                      ,

        ,

        .   amount   suffice   transcend
physical state.   ,   crate,
        .

        ?

    uncover mystery .

                              |
                              V
....
....>>>>>>>>>>>>>>>>>>>>>>>>>>>>
<
                        [ends: keeps]

THIRTEEN.

" :   daily ..."
    "?"
    ",,   wake   morning? ?   ,   ,   ?"
    Strange .   .   : ", afraid unacceptable."   .

      ", :   ?"
      ", !   ."
      "   ?"

      "   ?   guess.   . –   somewhere,   –   .
anywhere,   . rode   couple . while   , tried   .
everywhere stopped, couldn't   .   stops . obvious.
plan,   evaporated desert heat .   , completed circuit,
recognized   gotten .   – . , ..."

      , , , exactly she'd .   , :

Religion   motivational/   sports   sex   crossword
puzzles board   occupying exercises   successfully
Conspiratorial   . . hoax spiritual attainment, con   benefits
purity (near-)sinlessness , wonderful motivations.

.B.

image   haunts .   .   .   affect ?   scene?   .   .
reaction overcame evening.   quashed.   losses , self.
render vulnerable, vulnerability behoove . erase aberration
.   ,   deal .   fight   .

XIV.

", writer?" disturb.   , black, , bother .... sneaking
suspicion   ... what's   ?   ?

      " ?"
      " , correct?"
      "Incorrect."
      ,   mentioned   .   .   , "   ?"

“ writes.”

“... definition, , ... *writers*   , twisted breed, exploit , defined . ... *art.*   .   ?”

“ form expression.” , quick book teachings.   . attended.

“Bullshit.   – .   combat –”

“?”

“ inner ...” lose train .   pouring coffee onto .   . ,   .   poured hits. Kicks tad.

“ interrupt ....” rarely   saying, ,   ...

“Originally, discussing   .”

nuts.   grasp?   fix mentally deranged ,   sane insane. ,   , ...   ,   utilizing extraordinarily . ,   astray, temptress   tragic hero. Albatross!   stick   ride, confident , .   ,   ignorance deteriorate .

,   verbal communicator , . speaker,   . hears,   . .   . aren’t listening.

“ ,   misrepresented, misinterpreted, , misinformed, mystified.   , turf .   .

“ ”
 , ,

“List ,” ,

“ stem,” ,

“ , ... ” ...

“?”

“ ?   .   .”

childhood . kind illness ? parents,   ? incubated birth ,   larger, metaphorical, incubator?...   bring ... ...

JYGYLDYK.17.

superspace . .   windowsill, realizing , window .
Luckily, purchased - protection .
           , ? spaces . Unnerve. , crap. .   fountains. . .
types reasons,   . move . ?
          park   large space   enclosed structure   bazaar.
extended interior hallway... ears imbalanced.   ceilings

illuminate   hallways buzzing rays penetrate   infest   hum-
hum-hum   , unfailingly inducing intense anxiety   . ...
                eyeglasses ,   bought frames   years .
identification .   invites opposite .   minutes,   ,   .   .
irritated.

                   ?

   .

          forgotten ?
            doing, ?

          ?
          dozed ?
            ?
            ?
          ?

             ?   ?   ?
          eternal ,   .

          "   ?" blurt . "   .   ! . !"   , aback amused
ridiculousness.
                ,   . quickly impropriety   , explaining   hung-over,
operates unusually   drinking – circuits ,   –   . takes
convince   . Eight , , "   ."

          proceeds   blood   . , silently, . spend   .

FIFTEEN.

crowded .

old,

           clings
           sags ,

                          suspended

      ,

      ,

         .

   .

   sleeping,   .   food,   ,   .
rectum,
      ,   .   wipe ass.
                 inescapable incontrovertibles,   facts, , ,
weaknesses, vulnerabilities,   unavoidable helplessness,
humanness.   ,   . annoys.
         /   ?   ultimate unanswerable,   ?

                                                    ,   .

18.

                 ...   hide,
           smaller hole closes
         ;
      , , surround.
         ,   -
      enveloped   .
      ,,, dig-
ging....
         implode.........

narrow, claustrophobic
    ,   strive

dimmer…....................

XIX.

girls,   . , , performance   implausible   .   cry.
likewise ,   avail. efforts , leads   .

"you'll
            "

output   worth input.   ?   ?   ?   ?   ?   ?   ,
…   ?

TWENTY.

FOrty . : 3 ;( ):

1.   himself,   .

2. "   .   .   massaging.   molesting ."

3. ",...   ,   ,   .   painful , ,   .   , ugliness
hidden, pain tolerable –   feeling   ."

30.

 ....

 ...

 "   soon."
 "   ?"
 "   questions robot   ."
 " ?" referring   scratches   bridge   experience
maddening   scratched   ... .   fac.e,,,;;.

.

 " since ." .   . . " ?"   N.
 .   . fail. .   replace .   looked ? tt .   ss.   ?
.

begin   .   .   sound .   ,   . b somehow
converse

"   predestination?"
      ?   .   .
"insofar   predestined . ,   box nails... house...
hammer... wood..."

grows louder. surrounds   .   clouds.

sick   .   :

.s.l.o.w. . . . .
. . . .
. . . . .t.i.l. . . .m.o.o.n.l.i.g.h.t.s. . . . .
.m.e.m.o.r.y.

                  chest
 .   .   .   .

                rupture
      heathens   .   pits .

          jump
      acid   s. ? .   .
            .
                idead.
            y   ou   ,
            wh n   ,
nd ths b ,
 son   ,   d d.

.

" hadn't   .   —   exploded ,   ?   , guilt.
,   ,   .   ."

            dreams. ,   — apology, treaty, gift, bone thrown.
Catch, bitch!
            , dream

*canvas, painting, working diligently, focused . stands
middle   floors walls , windows opening clear skies,
roof .   raised stilts lake// -   wooden poles.
,   days   —   remains blank.   strokes   .   , ...;
.   angle;   object   sides   , standard dreamscape ...   .   —
, , .   ,   .*

    piece — marked   paint.

Dr. , ?

.

!.

?.

... .

"   ?"

"?" ;   moved   stagnant reverie... " —... um, ,   ..."
       pack   cigarette.   , logo resting atop, .   . habit,

.

"   ?"

" ," shrug. " .   ? . ,   ."
", telling. affected , , worried ,   ."
offers compelling explanation...
       "   ?"

   sorts,   visions apparitions illusions ghost

...

places,   –
  –

  (?) .
  picture
vividly,
– uninvited – associate feelings   imaginary landscape.
     . visual ,

  cognition   superb, surreal, .
     ?
?   , outside
  imagination?   ?   ?
     grant ,   measure relative ?   myster-
ious memories
implanted   disc pd=t   ... spontaneous hallucinations...
determining

          .

     ?
  fake?
                ?
          context negatively configured?
          ?
          ( )
greater value?
          faced   matters,
   versus   valuable .   ?
                (t)here permanently?

?

       recurring   .

   ... ,   .

                            −
      city,   −
      ,
      cars, , sounds .

      , ,   buildings .
      ,   ,   approaching, stealthily (contradiction   dream-logic),

   .

both
 dreaming   dream-self,
actor   director,
   spectator,

     ,   .

            confront   second −

      spin   slides knife   tearing flesh   blade
      −   except :   gone, dreaming-self .

      .

         .   , , . streets .

       .   ; , ,   hurt   stabbed.   odd, indescribable...   ... −
   −   − bleed,   . , .   bleeds? . Sharp ,   . Blackness   .
Flashes , .   ?

         . .   .   .   .   .   sidewalk. . .

                                                          trance,
         .   infected.   , burns , innerwhelming gulf   floods
      fire   precedes resignation.   bleeding   suffering
      ... false sympathy.   ,   , , ,   breaths caring single   ,

sprout

,

,

wondering   kicked ,   bruised   hit,
   breathe   choking,
      silenced,

         .

            owe   .   forgive ,   ,   ; , accurately,   .   . :
   .   ,   accord ,   vastly . ?   −   ,   .   ,   practicing
 −   ,   worst.   , stab .   hundreds
         ,   ,   ,
,
   quicker pace,

,

               trench coat   stabs silver   grabs

      disappears,
  pool
 ,
      .

turns corner ,
celerity −

         .

      .

   ,

        running   circles,
suddenly jumping   ,

                              circle formation
                  ____
                  ||| <<<< >>>> |||
                  || <<<< locks >>>> ||
                  ||| <<<< >>>> |||

                  ||||| <<<< . >>>> |||||

    ,   ,

tighter

          thicker

...   .

                    |||=>>> <<<<=|||
                         \\V//
                         \\\ ///

 .

    :

          scream

(lucid   irrelevant   )
continuation   Error   :::

greatest, , flaw   tendency becoming overexcited discoveries advancements   overlook details implementing .   −   − . , ,   calculate perfection procedures repercussions .   , thrive.

aforementioned ????.   instance,   , alien infiltrating   corrupting . ,   − recall   invasion, gratuitously named Scare, −   miserably,   easily   . (, , , died   thirty .   thrilling UFO sighting   incredibly anti-climactic.)

???? ... ?   . mistakes. (?)   incidence , aliens assimilated , appearing , resultantly   . ,   evidence support theories sufficiently. ,   :

, overwhelmed glee sheer concept Employment Task Assurance (, recognizing),   grave deviations projected .   Cresteds ( ) managed infiltrate materializing , Nation-born citizens,   compensate .
- .

,

pre-calculated   unemployed   declared Vital ( ), .   , propound ???? , propaganda − cover covering , involving sort concord   Crested .

tend credence latter; ,   written − muddled, "paranoid" conjectures   endless thinking. claims presenting utter herein;   document   occurrences , seeing , infinitesimal , generation , drastic cataclysm, , ,   -. , - Herb Morrison ,   sky .

:

                                              throat
,   oasis . senses ,   . jolt   cough, "Excuse,"   . brace
wall, accidentally putting   frame   shatters   pressure .
dog licking paws puppy golden-haired   watered   lean
grass tall   shoe .
              you'd   .   embedded   paw.
              hall   stumble   drunkard's conviction   bull   ring
summer   glares egg sand   beast,   ,   lunges

                    vomit climbs sideways   horrid expulsions
waste   rebelling   metal bottom stall divider clench
desperate futility sweating   claps   swelling   cranium
forcing   cracking

shaking
 climbing
                        scattering
                          tiles
 sweat   wanting
shrieks
 cries
 violent nightmares   burn

 .

23.

    , gasping   infrequently
      .

screaming.

.

.

.

4OUR.

. ; , .   ,   suffer. ,   . , k .

     , , : legs stronger, thighs muscle, stamina , -
kick   flows bruises   .

, invincibility,
fatality...

bed lie,

sheets

.

building,

,

,

s

harnessed,

, knowing

wai t
 blankness
 whiteness

,

monitors visible
   theire .

   Core

disguise

  minions

 leans
smell stank
whispers devilishly
"   prime "

  original , fucker.
    , .
"madness   ,"
   freak.

"   selfs.
   madman,

     .

  pigeon."

.

    ,
     ,

  ,
  ,
  ,
  ,

   void.

 inject
serums cancers diseases,

   dance,

,
  nights unable ,

companion,
 torment,
  tumble
  , toss
aimlessly, chaotically,
infecting, spreading,
eating   stability, . solidity,
 ( )

.

        ,

          ,

       ;

)[6]

"   ,   ?"
                    ...   ...
          ...   .
"...   ,   !"

                          '   ˙
.   -   '   /   ([,
]),   .

                              .

20 .

  . .

        dispatched , returned   peace . inhalation, . sat
couch   , , , months, .   . intoxicants immobile,   , .
abilities,   terrible shot   . .
       . opponents strong weak;

:

.

, result checkmate.

self-evident.

.

organs , weigh corpse, fill lining, ,
, *mon corps*, core, ,
, , , innards, inners,
.

deny .

      .

         .

   .

   seek.

.

      "   ? ? . *740 , 3033.   1968. 82.   ?   ?*
deliberately confusing   –   ,   cease . defying ,
forever.   , - ( ) – temporally situated?   beginnings .
goal.   infinitely infinity .   ?"

.

         ?
            . , ... ?   ?   fit
puzzle?   passive reactionary   ?
      .
      . – .   possibilities , , exists .

, .

         extra,   runoff   message cast   , disowned,
fucked   forgot   sum   added mistake   subtract erroneous
unit nonplussed surplus

extinguished
  effete constant meaningless contemplation

                                                        , ,

process

installation t   /

                                                    hot

cold

                                                    supplied

chemical

balanced …

spared faulty   ruin

unless replaced   fits   closing   discarding

                                                 terminate
d

                                                 erase

                                                d

beca

caca

d

    symbol   failure

    admitting

    inferno

        sunny
    shadow
      disappear

        cleaning crew

    clean

  , ,
  final plea

  posing   constructed deserve   answers

asphyxiated

hurriedly

limp lifeless
incinerated

w a s t e   .

XX VIII.
library
humiliating

(beating drums   marching band)

eats

tapeworm psyche

. young
locked

.

,

.

neighbor's .   ,   .   ,   ,   doors, . Stuck ,   ,
. panicked,   pants.

.   .   .   .

XXIX.

| received   , accusing numerous offenses, slandering name
portraying various incidents. policemen. Inspectors   insulted.
court date   attend.   demand   –   , invite   ; ,   …
captive,   …   protect …'ve   ,

.

" hearing   ?" judge . balls. 've   . !   holes
faces   controlled …   awaits response.   .   ?   .
.   happening ?
"."

"   ?"

. nice , whoever   . "   . suffered ,   .   ."
"   ?"

".   .   .   ,   obligations   ordinary
capacity   functionally   adequately .   ,   ."

"   charged theft, trespassing, possession , intent, assault, conspiracy, violation orders, accounts …-"
"?   ?"   hopeless .   .   . !!!   !   –"
treat , ?   , ,   .   ,   .   fought   complained fulfilled   , reward behavior moving , darker cell, , .   ?"

.

.

        burden   brought

"   defecate   tormenting

–."

→ lowest vilest   ruined

XXX.

" starving , ,   plate rests table.   hunger;   .   .
, , . starve   .   ; ,   , .   .   .   ,   . .
."

:

                    ...

.

defense

                              reassurance

                    ETF plans

                              "
'?'
"

                              ***

          ", , sir ,
                              "   practiced .
"

"

"

                                                                    ' '

                                                    ENTIVES
                                                        "

...

push   .

EPITAPH EPITHETS.

blow ,   . gums   howl   , knuckles   prudent
reduce injury.   ,   .

          , relief – .   .   . ...

     .   . Rethink.
     ? let's   beginning...

          ,   .   ⁻ , .   , ,

moments   scribble drivel

: anxieties – physically manifested –   exterior.

. , screwed.

, inundated diluted, futile obsessions;   ,   sanctuary
.   covered   ,   lucky, ,   ,   .   . darkness proves
shade ;   .
seven   unleash. unsure   convictions opinions –
.   phrases , restlessness…   exhaustion cool .   wanted .
distractions .   ,   .   driven ,   purge.
Tangibility . escapes   bars,   .

, friend,   .

A Note from the Editors

After the author's death, police investigators conducted a routine search of the victim's apartment. The official report, released months later, stated that the search produced no valuable evidence regarding the case at hand – with the exception of the following discovery (as quoted from the report):

> ...Police Inspector _________ noted various scraps of paper scattered about the premises, which were collected and later analyzed at headquarters. The handwriting was confirmed to be that of the victim's, who was some kind of writer; the papers were determined to be his working notes...
>
> Some of these notes are of great interest to the case...[because they] describe the murder of a character, planned and executed in manner nearly identical to the actual murder of the victim... Both killings...almost exactly the same...[in terms of the] murder weapon, number of times stabbed, scene of the crime, even time of day and weather. These striking similarities are curious and hard to explain, and may shed some light on the culprit's identity...

However intriguing, the discovery failed to bring the officials any closer to identifying and arresting the murderer. Ultimately, the court ruled that the writings were "inadmissible as evidence."

Soon after, the investigation was dropped altogether, quietly and easily for the lack of public interest and private concern.

Once the case had officially closed, the Editors contacted the police department and requested copies of the victim's notes. As we were already working on the publication of the first edition of *New Roses*, we were curious about these writings.

Within weeks, a shoe box-sized package arrived, full of some hundred scraps of scrawled-upon paper. Upon analysis, we realized that we had just received the raw, un-edited material for an intended second section of *New Roses*.

We took the liberty of organizing the notes into a coherent whole, attempting as faithful a construction as possible. We refrained from making any changes to the actual prose, and chose to include everything that we received from the authorities.

The result is included below.

-the Editors

NEW ROSES.

the flowers bloom.

there were snakes in the bathroom
and they slid across the floor,
vanishing under the blue floor mat
slipping between the cracks
where the walls met the linoleum.

i stood in the doorway and glimpsed
a light brown black speckled rattler –
then another appeared from under the sink,
dark brown with patterned triangles
and diamonds of a lighter brown.

anxiously my feet scattered across the floor,
fearful cautious; and with two light steps
i landed in the bathtub.

i stood in half a foot of water.
there were no snakes in the tub,
for which i felt very grateful.

the tub was white.

i noticed no shower curtain.

: MD   BRAIN METABOLIC IMAG/PET

Attending Physician: , MD
Associated exams:

History: Nuclear medicine was consulted to evaluate regional brain function in this…patient with medication refractory behavioral dysfunction. Specifically, the goal was to determine if an occult seizure focus could account for the lack of responsiveness to conventional therapy. No other information was known at the time of this assessment. No anatomical images were available for direct correlation.

Technique: High resolution tomographic images of the brain were acquired after the intravenous administration of 2.93 mCi of [F-18] FDG according to standard operating procedures. The patient assented, documented in writing.

Findings: The results showed widespread brain dysfunction in the left cerebral cortex that was significantly more extensive than the left temporal lobe. The metabolism in the right medial temporal lobe was abnormally decreased. Otherwise, the right hemisphere appeared intact. The diencephalon seemed to be largely spared.

Impression:
This study showed extensive left hemispheric dysfunction. An ictal focus could not be definitively excluded as contributing to the pathophysiology, but something more than simple TLE is operant.

I certify that I have personally reviewed this examination, and agree with this report.

Approved by:
                 , MD   /signed by/

COPY

It is now night, or early evening.

The streets get dark early these days.

I sit here in my apartment. It is dark in my space but for the light of the small lamp on my desk where I write.

Outside, the wind is strong and the air is cold. The window to my left is thin and cracked, inviting the winter chill in. The radiator in the back corner of the room works hard to keep me warm, exclaiming its effort with coughs and clanks and screams and steam.

A drop of water just hit this page. Reflexively, I looked up at the ceiling; water, condensing on the exposed pipe above me, gathers to drip. I sit back and observe the process: the initial moisture surfaces like beads of sweat on skin; they grow, slowly, gradually swell, proliferate, subsume surrounding beads, accumulate, and collect along the underbelly of the pipe. Here they wait, patiently, for their moment to succumb to gravity, to freely slip drip down and descend, like one determined drop of rain, to land upon my desk, to be followed by others, continually, in measured, deliberate, compounded frequency. (This phenomenon, at this particular moment, transcends its situational singularity to suggest something infinite and everlasting. The sublime power presented me, the awesomeness of the natural, has momentarily sublimated all other thoughts, successfully occupying me for a brief eternity. Unfortunately, I return.)

Six years have passed since I last sat down to write, including the four years I languished in prison. For six years, though, I have glided along listlessly, senselessly, thoughtlessly. Now I find myself feeling lost; and I feel that I have nothing left but the exercise of writing to help me understand who I am, why I am, where I am. And so, after so many years, I return to the written word, to try and figure out where I am right now.

I have no expectations or prescribed direction in mind. I'm writing because I need to – not because I want to. If *the Truth* represents my past, then what will come to be this section will present my present. These are the notes of my mind.

I like my apartment – it is preferable to many other places I've been.
My room here is small, but I do not feel caged or afraid.

■■■

I am uncertain as to the truth of anything asserted in the first section of this book. I find this realization – or acknowledgment, perhaps – mildly disconcerting, but not surprising. I have never trusted anyone – certainly not myself.
But at the same time, I find it interesting that the previous writings prefigured the actualization of the events they described. Before I knew it, I really was in court, and then in prison. By that point, I had already completed writing *the Truth*.
In other words, that which I wrote ended up writing me: the pen led the way.
The question is, then, Did I foresee my arrest, my trial, my imprisonment? Was it perhaps my anxious predictions that sculpted my future, meaning, presently, my past?
Every event I encountered was curiously cloaked in a blanket of déjà vu.
I've been here before...
All I can say for sure is that it is difficult for me to say what is true and what is not true, because whatever memories I retain exist as doubles – mirrors of visions that sometimes reflect the same image, sometimes project different views.

■■■

The one fact I do know is that I spent three years and seven months inside, behind bars, where my world was gray gray gray. I have documentation of this.
Looking back at the last chapter of *the Truth*, I can't help but think to myself, What a load of shit. I don't understand how my obsessions were "diluted," unless he meant it as a play on

"deluded," which is acceptable. However, I must admit that the last passage possesses an unwonted clarity largely absent from the majority of the text.

Regardless, it's always dangerous to think you know what you're talking about. You can convince yourself of anything.

■■■

I considered retouching parts of *the Truth* with various details and explanations, but decided against it in order to preserve whatever imaginary truths may be found therein, which in any case ought to be more interesting than the actual truth. So it remains as it was.

■■■

It was January when I got thrown in. January, like it is now. Six years ago.

I wanted to open the window to feel the cold air outside, though I was already shivering jittery. And sweating, too, though it wasn't hot.

The window in my cell was small and barred, square, with two-inch thick glass just beyond the bars. Through this limited frame I made a small lot below, a triangular courtyard located within the center of the prison compound. The area was formed by three inverted walls, two of which did not meet to allow a driveway for official vehicular access. A sometimes truck was parked adjacent the loading dock. Though I never saw the truck move, sometimes it was not there.

Whenever I'd notice its absence, I would imagine it exiting through the narrow passage, into the vast expanse of the free world; likewise, when I looked again and it was back, I'd envision its entrance, returning to its resting place within the confines of the dead gray womb of the inner compound.

One thing about this space: the pavement, the truck, the loading dock, the prison walls, the little bit of the beyond that I could just barely make – everything, all of it, was gray.

■■■

I spent almost four years inside that building. Not in that exact room, of course. They put you in quarantine first, and after ten days or something, you're moved into the pods.

     I used to think that maybe, if I ever ended up doing time, it wouldn't be that bad. It would give me the opportunity to spend every waking hour reading and writing. Maybe I'd even work out a little, get in shape – who knows! With all that time on my hands...I could get so much shit done... In a way, it's the writer's dream – no distractions whatsoever...just peace and quiet...focus of solitude...and plenty of time. How much writing I could accomplish!

     It's very naive to carry an idealized perception of prison. In fact, it's very stupid. Now, from experience, I know better; I know that I never want to spend another day in there ever again. And I promise you, myself, that I won't.

     It's not that my time in prison was terribly traumatic or psychologically scarring; I managed to stay out of trouble – as miraculous and unbelievable as that may sound. My pain came in the shape of the clock, for mine was to be, quite characteristically, the torture of time. It is in this sense that I view my incarceration as absolutely inhumane and horrifying, and it is with the deepest and most extraordinary contempt that I regard my time inside. My punishment was the horror of the reality of the boredom of the indeterminate chain of indistinguishable days...the suffering through which quashed every ounce of my creative intellect – my only quality of value, all that I cherish and respect of myself. The timeline of the damned, the dehumanization of categorical subjugation, the interminable string of twenty-four hour shifts of unchanging routine, the blank walls that face you from every direction, all served to smother any desire I had to write, extinguish any spark of inspiration, and wholly rob me of myself. With that, reality, all my illusions of constructive use of time in prison vanished.

     When I was booked, I received an eraser – but no paper, no writing tool.

So, I worked with what I had.

....

Two years have passed since my release from prison, since the
expiration of my temporal sentence to institutional incarceration,
since I was refunded the privilege of my "freedom" and handed a
signed, stamped, approved, and very official-looking piece of
paper to prove it.

When I first got out, I had no idea what to do with myself.
One might think that four years would be enough time to figure
something out, formulate a plan, set some goals. But no.
Nothing. In fact, the entirety of my years inside was wholly
unproductive; I experienced no epiphanies, no revelations, no
moments of self-realization; no insight, no inspiration. These
years, to me, are an empty void. I left that place with nothing but
blanks.

I moved back to my old house, pretending not to recognize
it, for the health of my head. I spent a lot of time cleaning, fixing
it up from the many years of neglect it had endured...throwing out
old shit...trying to give it the appearance of something other than
that which it had been before. This work, ranging from menial
tasks to more physically demanding labor, filled the time of the
days and gave me a much needed sense of purpose, false or
otherwise.

I got a job at a local bookstore. I mowed the lawn.

Sometimes I would sit and think about the years of my life
leading up to my imprisonment. The details were difficult to
situate. My mind would wander through hazy imaginings of
certain places and things...territories, both physical and
psychological, that I found impossible to distinctly map... I
cannot describe them here. Each time I try, I fail. Like explaining
a dream, at the very moment of the formation of a verbal relation
– *everything* disappears. Psychic suggestions of movements of
clouds across my mindscape, all that remains, handicapped
reconstructed experiences.

Sometimes I would sit and think, allowing my mind to entertain imaginings of future Encounters I may face. Sometimes I would sit and think about whether I should sit and think...especially about Encounters...and about the nebulous mist that I can scarcely grasp that is my life before prison. After all, those days have already been represented in *the Truth*. And, as I had been instructed several times by my judge, my counselors, and my PO, I should put that shit past me.

I knew, I could recognize, that I felt better. I was less anxious, less angry, less depressed, less emotionally unstable...one can recognize these things.

But the consciousness of my past tendencies towards these behavioral characteristics, and the acknowledgment that the psychological and chemical foundation that berthed these problems (such fertile soil, nurturing the healthy growth of the seeds of disorder) still existed within me and continued to occupy a place in my mind, haunted me. The threat of a full-fledged return to the torture I had endured before...caused me great worry. It was an issue I could never fully overcome. To some degree, this horror plagued me continuously.

In my mind, I gave it the form of a simple white ghost, imaged like those found in children's books. This ghost followed me everywhere, hovering above and behind me, ever-ready to pounce, seize my body, and bring me down all over again.

I was curious about how closely I was being watched, so I tried to be straight, responsible, as respectable as I could manage. I found myself neither satisfied nor dissatisfied. I just was. My mind was a blank canvas, intentionally, for my own safety. No ambitions, no ideas of what I should do. I felt only emptiness. This mental state plagued me, a vestige of my reaction to prison.

At the bookstore where I worked, the people talked, and I kept my mouth shut. I spent most nights at the bar, by myself, floating in the solace of a lonely liquid retreat after an exhausting day dealing with people.

After a year of this stagnation, I decided I ought to move. Legally, I was finally able to. So I did. I moved.

And now, I live in the city.

It always takes time to be able to look back. When I reread *the Truth*, it is clear to me that the writer was looking ahead too much, which is not only retarding but counter-productive and unhealthy.

I recognize in that piece of writing a plea for external anarchy matched with an intense internal instability that defined the few years of his life prior to my imprisonment. Chaos is what he wanted, and ultimately what he achieved.

Anyway, I couldn't resume writing after my release from prison. At first, I couldn't find *the Truth*, partly because I never deliberately searched for it. When I finally did locate my writings – tucked away underneath a heap of dirty laundry in an old chest in the attic – I was very excited. Upon reading it, however, this excitement deflated into a heaping pile of stifling stinking malaise. The emptiness that had become a part of me during my years in prison still occupied me, and prevailed. I simply didn't care. I had no interest in writing, no desire.

This was probably for the better: Following my release, a process of restabilization was necessary, which proved much more challenging than my destabilization, which was easy and, in retrospect, felt quite natural and good.

But yet, so I tried, and so I (believed) achieved, in a way...all the while keeping to myself whatever convictions I maintained. During this time I controlled myself...I stayed quiet, withdrawn but present, superficially playing along with their crazy games – but never forgetting that the apparatus subsists on forced notions of proper realities, absurd projections of health and normality, functional (therefore acceptable), cultivated anxieties and privileged insecurities and simple gratifying morality, achievable ideals of success, facile platitudes of expected, proper emotional behavioral exhibited allowances; affordable comfort; all such inane, imposed indoctrinations of this our super-reality...useful social mechanisms, borne of the tumultuous marriage of natural human inclinations towards conflicting (oppositional/contained combustion) engaged aptitudes for unnaturally developed pride and self-loathing, megalomaniacal obsequiousness, jealousy and contempt.

My psychiatrist enjoys contending that the initial shock of incarceration resulted in my retreat to a less psychotic state (however slight, however paradoxical), that the trauma and emotional distress of being uprooted and replanted on alien soil, foreign, intimidating, and oppressive, plus having to kick, triggered a reflexive, instinctual, self-preservational response, an animalistic survival mechanism.

I agree with him. But I find his insipid smile, whenever he asserts this point, distasteful and pathetic – the look of someone who has just discovered some brilliant truth and is straining to conceal his self-satisfaction.

He's also afraid that this mechanism may simply constitute a psychological block, a wall erected to deal with this immediate shock, in order to protect me from the reality of my position, a reflexive hardening of self to prevent a total breakdown, a wall that threatens to collapse at any moment.

This also seems perfectly reasonable to me.

I distinctly remember the night I was booked, one thirty in the morning.

Before going to prison, I had to first meet with the D.A. I sat in the courtroom, flanked by the two cops with whom I'd spent the last ten hours – true heroes, for sure. The big man finally arrived to do business; sober and well-rested, and of clear and composed mind, within minutes he capably judged me for what I was: a schizoid serial law-breaker, criminally conspiring against the law of the land (an illegal conspirator, if you will). As a Representative of the Good and the Safety of the State of the Nation, he declared me a "serious threat to the harmonious order of our Great Nation," and demanded immediate incarceration of my body, without bail.

The two cops escorted me to the prison, handed me over to the facility's corrections officers, and took their leave of me. I felt a slight tear in the air as they parted, as if we had grown close over the course of our time together.

First, I was placed in a large cage with a handful of other unluckies, where we were all welcomed with a brown bag of "edibles."

I couldn't touch the shit food out of that shit brown bag that was shitted out for the incoming shits. I can't even fully remember what it was exactly, a poor sandwich I think, some colored sugar water, and a side of chemical cardboard – I don't remember no but just that it was fucking nasty and I couldn't do more than look at it let alone touch it let alone eat it after that first bite.

Then individually summoned, so for to commence the booking process rigmarole...

I had had nothing up my rectum, so no problems there.

I was weighed and mug shotted and numbered and after listening to the listing of my personal possessions I was handed the bright orange INMATE GUIDELINES and the gray blue INMATE DISCIPLINARY PROCEDURES handbooks and forwarded along to the medical examiner...with whom I was not yet prepared to deal.

It was two-thirty in the morning by the time I finally graduated from the bureaucracy, peaced the process, and made my bunk. Thirteen hours after being pulled over, I was finally in a cell...

My cell-mate greeted me, moaning unpleasantly; he was three days in heat, kicking the shit. A nasty sight, but better than other imaginable housing partner situations.

Three days without...needless to say, he wasn't doing well.

This is what happens.

We all know this.

And I knew that this was going to happen to me, soon enough.

And I knew that the only thing I could do, the only thing there was for me to do, was wait.

I didn't sleep at all my first night there.

▪▪

But now I work, just like you.

In an office, in a building, in the city, here.

I've been out for over two years now. I've been in the city, and at this job, about a year now.

I'm good at seeming normal, straight. Most of the time. I keep to myself.

I feel no connection with my co-workers. No force draws me near them. They exist merely as strangely animated objects.

▪▪

Maybe it's the grays that I grew accustomed to that prompted me to move to the city.

But also, the suburban wasteland of green and white became too much for me to handle – too many shadows lurking behind the trees, beyond the light of the projector.

And although resettling to the city may not seem like the best move for an anxious psychotic who suffers paranoid nightmares of being stabbed in the back on a city street, I find living in the city to be quite calming.

▪▪

I hardly remember anything of my youth. I don't retain any true memories, access denied, at best only fleeting moments of guesses at self-knowledge, a designed imagined past of questionable veracity. Memories involve sight more than anything, I think, though maybe this is not true.

My point is that I see nothing. Occasionally I can just barely grasp certain images from my past – but they are clouded, dimly lit, ethereal. Nothing tangible, nothing to hold on to, nothing truly credible.

The only certainty I possess is that at some point, when I was very young, I started drinking and didn't stop. My intention was to forget everything that had occurred around and within and to and by me. In this sense, I can confidently assert, I did a great job – it worked pretty well. Pretty well. Not perfectly, of course. Because my bastard brain likes to bust my balls.

▪▪

My work is dull. I'm doing it. I get paid.
Most days, I sit in front of the computer all day.
Day after day.
Mornings I wake up, I shower, I shave, I smoke a cigarette if I can, I drink some coffee if I have time. Shirt and tie. And out the apartment and down the stairs, outside, onwards and to the subway to a building to an elevator to an office where I sit and stare at a computer screen. All day long. For an average of nine-ten hours a day; five days a week, fifty weeks a year. Now, having been subjected to systematized torture before, this strikes me as a very effective form of dehumanization. Such a routine, which is evidently common and socially acceptable, seems like absolute madness to me – a sure way to drive anyone out of his mind. If nothing else, a practical apparatus of control.
And so I sit at my desk and dream fantasies of wondrous ecstasies of warmth, the flood the rush the deep warm red perfection of feeling.
And every morning I wake up from the dream of another liquid high to the concrete reality of another day at work and I think about how much easier it would be to tie my tie so tight that my head turns purple and falls off.
It's a curious image – I laugh with my self in the mirror and then we bend down to tie our shoes.

▪▪

A shot of whiskey to whet the old appetite. Now I should be able to swallow my lunch. It's funny how that works, a force with paradoxical powers. Drink can prevent me from eating, yet drink can remind me that I need to eat. Wonderful, no?

Some shrill-noted bird at work was screeching about her alcoholic grandfather, "He *rarely* eats anything. Of course, when *I* get drunk, *I* eat a *ton* – it helps with the hangover the next morning, you know! But my grandfather, he *never* eats *anything*, and he drinks a *whole bottle* of vodka a day!"

He probably drinks more than that, especially when you're around, I thought to myself. Of course, I kept my mouth shut, said nothing (my characteristic reaction; sometimes I wonder why people talk to me at all – I never say anything). I can't stand people who speak with excessive inferred italics and obnoxiously palpable exclamation points.

It all comes down to need, fueled by desire. When one is an alcoholic, alcohol takes precedence over everything, including food. Food is hardly a consideration. It's simply an after-thought, an inconvenience. At times, its necessity becomes painfully apparent. But most of the time – most of the time being spent drinking – it is not a concern. We worry about such superfluities only when they demand attention.

I have been drinking for as long as I can remember – literally. For me, this has been the most consistent and dependable drug. The pain it brings me is hard, but the life it gives me is all that I now know. The life...this is what I am here to consider...

■ ■

Over the course of my short life, I've been prescribed dozens and dozens of different medications - goofballs. Some of them I like, others I don't. But I'll try anything. I've always been very open when it comes to introducing chemicals to my body.

I still frequent a psychiatrist, who monitors my mental health. For what reason, I can't remember. Yet we continue our dance.

I have my ups and downs, and suffer the occasional unprovoked attack on my mind and my nerves, when the enormous empty shadow body, barely outlined, jumps out and grabs hold of me tightly to wrestle me down. Sometimes I take the drugs he gives me. Sometimes I don't take them, and come back to him with made up reports of adverse side-effects.

"Interesting," he'll say. "Well, let's try another approach..."

∎∎

What did I do wrong? I find myself thinking. Invisible hands beat my head.

What are you doing wrong?

I got caught.

Is that it?

Is that all?

I guess that's my fault. But it shouldn't be a crime. It's not. The crimes shouldn't be crimes. I was sick. This is bullshit. Stop.

∎∎

When I moved to the city, I applied to a temp agency. I needed a decent paying job, and I knew I could type well and handle secretarial work. Nothing glamorous, but within reach.

Filling out the agency's application, I got stuck on one question, and spent several minutes considering the appropriate response to: "Have you ever been convicted of any felonies or prior offenses?"

I had lied before on previous job applications, without a moment's hesitation. But this time I tripped. My criminal record, convictions and time served, is available in the Public Records. Anybody can access this information.

Either way I looked at it, checking yes box or no box, I was screwed. I could lie and check no, but they could easily conduct a background search, and I'd forfeit my chance of getting a job; or I could tell the truth about my record and they could turn me down on the spot. Both options carried risks.

But, I was trying to be good. My parole officer used to constantly remind me of this – of coming to terms with everything. So, finally, I figured, Fuck it, and checked the 'Yes' box.

The next week someone used a telephone to summon me to the agency's offices to discuss the possibility of employment; my criminal history was the first matter discussed. I think I played my part well.

"We all make mistakes," I explained from across the man's desk. I took a moment to establish direct eye contact with him (which I maintained as much as possible), and continued, "I wouldn't be sitting here before you if I hadn't already made a conscious decision to change my life for the better. I recognize my mistakes – I've had years to come to terms with them. I've served my time accordingly; justice has exercised its will; and, now that I've fulfilled the terms of my punishment, I wish to resituate myself as a functioning member of society.

"More importantly, perhaps, I now feel psychologically fit to enter the workforce, to reintegrate into society as a responsible, hard-working citizen. My year at the bookstore proves that I am reliable and can hold a job. If I find employment through your agency, I promise that I will perform my duties with the utmost diligence, professionalism, and respect." I paused for dramatic emphasis, leaned forward ever-so-slightly in my chair, and said, "All I'm looking for is a second chance. All I want is to put the past behind me – not to forget it, but to deal with it, and to get my life back on track."

The words were really terrible, and I don't know where they came from. But they worked. I gave him the number of my PO, whom I had also played well since my release. My term of reporting to him had expired, but I knew he would speak well of me, and I figured this would help my chances.

I shook hands with the man behind the desk, and then I exited his office.

No matter how hard I try, I have no recollection what the guy looked like.

I see all these people around me – in my office, on the street, in the bars – and I can't help but think to myself, Shit, these people are fucking insane.

Then I remember that I'm the crazy one – it's been determined. Scientific fact. I truly am "of questionable mental health." It is I who is the wrong. A bizarre thought to consider. Though certainly more bizarre for me than for you. You can just sit back in your comfy chair and say, Okay...

I don't know if I was supposed to feel differently about myself or the world after receiving the results of the diagnoses. Their diagnoses. I don't know what their intentions were. I still don't.

I don't consider myself crazy. Well, maybe I do. Yeh, no, I guess I do.

■■■

I'd like to say that I'm cured, that I'm happy, that I'm sane. But these words are meaningless. I wouldn't say some shit like that anyway.

Why should I be happy? Because I'm alive right now, because I made it through, because I'm here, now? Because of now? Because I didn't die and they didn't kill me?

Mere existence does not suffice in allowing me to assume a happiness – and as far as I can tell, my existence is the only thing I possess.

So I continue existing. That is all I can do.

My mental state remains relatively stable since it leveled during my imprisonment, since they forced their medicines upon me. But it fluctuates, with occasionally uncontrollable surges. I wonder about the effects of the new medication my psychiatrist prescribed. I still have difficulty reconciling the idea that I need to be medicated to be normal. This issue is incredibly problematic for me; when I struggle with it, I grow even more tired and depressed. I may stop taking everything soon.

■■■

I can admit that I took it too far.

You've read the first half.

Clearly, I took it too far.

Naturally, to a degree, I became the inevitable combined product of my choices, my lifestyle and my psychology; fueled by a near constant narcotic intoxication, with already present extreme chemical imbalances, poorly addressed by a myriad of influencing prescriptions. Pure madness, hedonism, and chemical sadomasochism. I feasted on a steady diet of anything and everything I could get my hands on. I wanted to escape the malevolent forces that surrounded me and physically crushed me from all sides. I wanted to escape to the *inside*, even though the inside was what tortured me the most. I thought that I could deny everything if only I could retreat within...to fight back, the war against...

Ultimately, I lost it – I lost control, I lost the war, I lost myself.

And they had me.

But is this an adequate explanation? Shouldn't I realize...should I think that they have me now?

∎ ▪

My chin feels bruised like I took a solid jab to the jaw last night.

I open my mouth and move my chin left and right, repeat, move it again with the guidance of my thumb and forefinger.

Strange.

I can't remember getting into a fight last night. I may have fallen, or bumped into something. But it's useless. I can't remember.

If someone had in fact punched me, I can't blame them. Sometimes I find that I can be the most annoying person in the world.

Maybe I fell again.

∎ ▪

I distinctly remember, the night I was booked, one thirty in the morning. I was arrested at one thirty in the afternoon, a detail noted only to indicate the inefficiency and incompetence of the stupid fucking pigs who ambushed and trapped and tortured me.

For the next twelve hours, chained to a precinct wall, I was a tense body of dread and anxiety and intensifying, urgent, unaddressed needs.

I sat there dumbly as they bombarded me with questions. They had caught me while I was driving. Then they had thrown me into their car, where they proceeded to yell at me, bent over, neck veins-a-bulging, disgusting. I could find no reason to respond to them. No justification whatsoever. They behaved like animals. Total idiots. Totally ridiculous. Instead of answering them, I asked my own questions; I demanded respect from them, and tried to warn them that they did not fully understand who I was, exactly – my place in the ---- of the -----. When they would not concede, I realized that I was dealing with the lowest form of drones the ----------- had ever created. The fools might not even be aware of the situation I was in, the situation that they were in.

Frustrated, confronted with the futility of engaging rationality against irrationality, I began cursing and swearing at the uniformed pawns, who only continued to lean over me with their dripping, fat sweaty faces and violent, rank offenses. Then I was struck.

When I regained consciousness, I found myself attached to the cement wall of a bleak room harshly lit by fluorescent overhead tubes.

I wanted a cigarette, I wanted a drink, I wanted a shot – a few codeines would've sufficed, for a time, or at least a handful of tranquilizers to help me cope with the oncoming nosedive of the dissipation of addictive substances my blood had become so dependent upon.

Most of all, I wanted to get the hell out of there.

I was full of fear. The clouds told me that I was had, that finally they had me, that they had me and they weren't going to let me go this time. Teeth clamped clenched around my neck like a shark-toothed noose, they had me and they were finally going to kill me. Silence me in some way. It all made sense. They'd been waiting. I guess I'd been waiting, too.

I saw no end in sight, no end in sight but the End. They were going to hole me up for life or kill me. Lobotomy, shock treatment, pd=t disc level extreme elevation. Torture. My fear was profound. Expectation does not equal preparation.

Of course, when you're in such a bad state – well, I kept grasping at unlikely possibilities like: maybe they'll let me out tonight and not take me in; then later: maybe if they un-cuff me from this bar on the wall I can make a dash for it, I can see a door over there...; and later: maybe the cops won't show up at the trial and I'll walk...; and then later: maybe I can escape from this courthouse...this prison...

None of these things happened. I can't say that I ever really believed they would. But I was desperate, and these fantastical dreams provided some comfort. If not for such dreams, I had nothing to look forward to.

▪▪▪

i tried to build
a house out of words
but the individual letters
could not stand on their own.

it was then that i realized
that words are not real.

▪▪▪

Today I had the opportunity to sit in front of the printer all day. I pressed a bunch of buttons a bunch of times. Occasionally I swiveled around in the chair there.

I'm tired of this fucking shit, my brain wired to my inner ears.

In truth, I'm beginning to think that my employment is some form of sentence, a type of highly engineered apparatus

designed and implemented to drive me absolutely insane – a
continuation of my punishment, no doubt. I wouldn't put it past
them.

▪▪

Pretty soon I'm going to focus on what's going on in my life right
now, which, although not necessarily of greater importance than
that which I relate of further temporal distantiation, should be of
greater relevance in the context of this section of *New Roses*, as it
might explain or illuminate why I'm writing this...why I'm
writing at all – why I've begun again. This of course suggests that
I am writing for a reason, which may be a faulty consideration.
There may be no valuable reason. But, if there is, what would it
be?
　　　Like I said, I've learned the value of looking back, the
practice of which helps me remember who I am, or who I think I
am, who I was (or think I was), who I could be, who I think I
should be now. To try to decipher who I really am. Am I still the
man in *the Truth*, or am I the man in *the Flowers Bloom*: newly
better, healthier, socially functional – a man with a job in an
office? My states need not be mutually exclusive, of course; I can
be both: was one, am the other. I've changed? It happens –
people change? Still I doubt.
　　　I can say this much, though, which counts for a great deal:
for the first time in my life, I can handle dealing with these
questions. They do not frighten or pain me as once they would; I
am able to consider such thoughts more thoroughly and with a
newly acquired calm.
　　　I'll give you some narrative progression soon enough.
Perhaps, though – just as a forewarning, just in case (...!...) – try
not to expect too much in character development.
　　　Just allow me a little more time to reflect...

▪▪

Motherfucker smelled bad. Constipated and releasing gas in those
tight constricted squeaks junkies squeak so well.

He screamed and cursed throughout the night. Hitting the wall, hitting the bed above him – where I lay, awake, hearing him, smelling him.

During his calmer spells, we spoke to each other. It wasn't easy, considering our conditions. But we managed when we could.

His name is Harold. When he said such, I nearly flinched – but managed to stay cool: naturally, I assumed he was a rat-stooge-plant-rat.

What kind of a name is Harold? I asked myself. It really sounded like something one of the ----------- had come up with as a joke – on me. He was a pigeon, no doubt, a fucking rat with wings, perched so as to keep an eye on me, to watch me and make sure I was... They would still need, after all, someone to perform this task...

But I soon gave up on this theory, and we became friends. I felt safe in letting my guard down, first, because he was definitely kicking, and second, because it didn't really seem to matter. I was already locked up. They knew everything they knew, and my talking to this being wouldn't change my position: I was had and they had me. The advantage was already theirs, plain and simple.

Looking back, I should state that I was lucky to have Harold as a cell-mate in the quarantine cells. I talked him through while he was kicking; he helped as he could when it was my turn. He was to be in for nine months. A regular guy. Probably an asshole. But a good guy, a regular guy. Construction, road work, manual labor; trucks, women, bars, meth, heroin.

Anyway, it's good to make friends inside. We had formed a bond early on that would help me greatly once I was in the pods. Without delving into his past, let us just say that he was well known. So, when I landed in the pods, it was well known that Harold and his crew would kill anyone who fucked with me. It's true: I was lucky. Really lucky. Because of his word, my safety was ensured – without having to pay any favors, without having to assert my strength, my toughness, my criminality. This protection

came from just being cool with Harold during his hard times. It
was important, he nearly begged, that no one know anything about
his condition in quarantine, that no one know about his habit. I
never spoke a word. So I was safe.

When Harold finally shit, the stench overwhelmed the cell.

■■

I know I drink too much. Much too much. It's not until I start
seeing double that I begin to recognize that I'm actually drunk.
        I've developed a solid dependency on liquids.
        You're talking about a man who's experienced some of the
greatest sensations known to the modern world. About a man
who doesn't know what the modern world means. About a man
who clearly needs something to be able to function in this world
of yours.
        Drinking helps me. It's the only thing I have left. The
only legal thing that gives me a sense of that fucked-up pleasure;
it helps me punish myself when I get to wanting. It helps me deal.
But I can never completely forget.
        Some memories you can never fully cover up...they may
disappear for some time, only to resurface...
        There's only so much you can do to forget.
        But so I drink heavily regularly.
        I'm destroying my balance, my liver, my brain. It's a
medicine that has serious side effects. But I see no other option.

■■

I remember
I lay in bed for a week
someone came to visit me
i think
i don't know who
i could barely see
but someone came
i know

to keep me alive.

why?

. ∎

I woke up this morning, sick. Again. I poured cheerios into my cup of coffee to try to eat something. It didn't make me feel any better. I looked at the clock and thought I might watch the news for a few minutes before work. I don't know why this thought occurred to me; I never watch the news – never turn on the tv before work. Very out of character, very strange.

I sat down on the couch and lit a cigarette to go with my coffee, black, two scoops of cheerios. I looked at where the tv used to be. It was not there. Only the lonely tv stand. I looked away and looked back.

It was still not there.

The screen would've reflected a look of confusion upon my face, were it there; although were it there, I would not bear that expression. I sipped my coffee and tried to think. I must've gotten really drunk last night, I figured to myself. I must have remembered...about the malignant ions that televisions emit. I used to keep my tv in the refrigerator, in my old house, to protect myself from the transmitter's negative energy. But I couldn't remember a thing from the night before...

I looked over to the kitchen.

Yup. There was the evidence.

The fridge was pulled out of its place, standing tall and awkward in the middle of the kitchen floor, circled a hundred times around with duct tape. I don't understand how I had failed to notice this when I was making coffee.

I looked back at the naked tv stand. I shook my head, not knowing what to do.

I got up and went to work.

. ∎

I wonder what time it is.

I bet it's almost six.

There's a clock on the wall, but I cannot see through the cubicle partition and I refuse to stand up from my chair to see above the gray quasi-wall.

Laziness, for once, is not the motivating force behind my lack of motivation. I wouldn't mind the act of having to get up. I just don't like the idea of that device controlling me.

I figure that the longer I postpone looking at the clock, the later it will be when I finally do. This notion gives me great pleasure. It could be six fifteen already! I could leave work in no time!

But if I look at the clock right now and it's only five, how disheartened I would be...

Of course, I'll have to look at the clock sometime this afternoon to avoid staying here longer than I have to.

For now, the gray partition = my friend.

■■

The jaws of fear, anxiety, swallowed me whole. The same shit that got me there in the first place. The last day, the last few days, the last months the last years. Scalping my head with a dull knife. Everything's in there.

And why am I here? Where am I? How did I get here? How did they find me? I thought to myself. I was no longer certain of anything.

My mind began to panic as it sensed my body's impending return to its natural state. I could hear the blinding fury of wild wings whispering indecipherably: having scoured the caverns of afar, they were returning to their home where the wind wails low, blowing past Time along the tributaries of my brain.

The sweats were coming on...

The guards advanced...

The battle was approaching...

War...

Even though there was nothing left to fight over – no meat on the bone, no bounty to loot, no territory to win, no power to usurp.

And so the clouds rushed across the gray night mind like a serpent across the surface of the dead sea in the universal orgasm.

∎ ▪ ∎

My sole possessions for four years ("any surplus items found in your possession will be confiscated as contraband and disciplinary action will be taken"):

    3 uniform shirts
    3 uniform pants
    4 underwear/briefs
    4 undershirts
    4 pairs of socks
    1 sweat shirt
    2 towels
    2 sheets
    1 pillow case
    1 blanket

This and only this – except the subsequent addition of a medical alert bracelet.

After a few days, my right arm started to swell. Sure, I was kicking. But this was another problem. Then, even worse, swelling occurred on the soles of my feet, manifesting as balls of tender, stretched flesh; whenever I stood, or walked, all of the weight of my body pressed down upon them. It was very painful.

Next my eye swelled shut, and that I could not hide or explain away. Which was probably for the better. I was transferred to the infirmary for a couple days, where there was a little more light and slightly better food. The environment was more pleasant than that of the holding tanks. I was treated like a patient and cared for, instead of constantly reminded of the unpleasant reality of being a prisoner. Moreover, Harold had already been moved to the pods; I was bound to get another cell-mate sooner or later, and who knows what I could've ended up with. I'd already gotten lucky once having harmless Harry at home. So again, this was better.

After a few days in sickbed, with the medications, the swelling reduced. I had also finished kicking. Everything was out of my system. I felt light, in limbo, lonely – not in the sense of lacking human contact/comfort, but in the sense of feeling empty, without. It was odd but somewhat pleasant, like feeling liberated when hopelessly lost.

I was then transferred to the pods, where Harold and his friends greeted me, with my new bracelet, as hospitably as their station allowed.

■■

My trial took place two weeks later. I couldn't understand a word of it, I couldn't understand what they were trying to do to me. It was as if the whole world had metamorphosed into a strange species of glossolaliating freaks, all wagging their fingers and shaking their heads at me in united disapproval.

The trial only served to further alienate me from any understanding of my situation. I began to doubt everything that I once knew so well, whilst simultaneously being handed confirmation of my paranoid convictions...

For a moment, I was even convinced that I myself may be one of the ----, that their influence was so strong that...

But then I was informed that the next four and a half years of my life were set canned, and I had no choice but to deal with this fact.

Over the course of the next few months or so (you may have realized by now that I have no comprehension of time – any reference to the passage of time is merely a feeble attempt at verbally gauging my loose perception of it, and is therefore arbitrary if not completely erroneous), my mind began to relax – slightly, incrementally.

The voices quieted down and backed off more and more, and I eventually grew accustomed to the daily routine of life on the inside.

I even began to breathe a little easier.

■■

Ah, Shit!

I realized my err the second I betrayed my concord with the gray object that was protecting me from the machine with the hands that cast spells of control like a sorcerer whose fingers spit chains!

My boss happened to walk by and – since I'd spent the last few hours in total befuddlement, making absolutely no progress with the work at hand – I jumped up to have a word with her, to try to get some hints.

And there it was, in plain view. With hubristic forbearance and malicious radiance it glared at me straight in the eyes and screamed "FOUR FORTY FIVE!"

How stupid and careless I was! I scolded myself, collapsing into my chair. I slumped there for a few minutes, trying to come to terms with my imbecilic action and diffuse my anger with myself.

My boss had continued on her way, without having noticed me at all.

∎∎

I can't focus.

Fuck the clock.

It was my fault, I know.

If I hadn't lapsed into a moment of supreme fucking idiocy just then, the clock might have finally smiled seven zero five when at last I mustered the courage to confront its blaze.

But what happened then was no act of courage. It may have been accidental, sure; nevertheless, such a self-defeating loss of self-control is unforgivable. I double-crossed myself, foiled my own intentions, dishonored my pact with the gray cubicle wall. Self-deceptively I was overcome, as if possessed by an uncontrollable urge of iniquitous depravity to deliberately defy my own worst enemy – me. For I am the enemy of my own self, as this incident proves. It is not you that I fear, or anything else that this awful world has presented me. It is my own self.

And alas, I am nothing. Nothing but a face fraught with nothingness, staring me down with hostile eyes that burn into mine.

And here I sit, a coward.

▪▪

This is prison.

▪▪

I just realized that *the Truth* makes no explicit reference to my love and use of opiates and other narcotics. I think it works better that way. But maybe she is in there. After all, this is just a meager attempt at situating some intangible truths amidst the brutal landscape of my personal psychological squalor and irrepressible mendacity born of pure uncertainty and innocent criminality. So I really can't be sure.

Anyway, as this is a separate section from *the Truth*, I can admit here the fact that profound drug addiction accompanied me along a good stretch of my life prior to my incarceration.

I have a long history of mental illness, and almost as long a history of drug use (some prefer the term "abuse"). Near-constant drug use, variegated for different purposes. But patterns in drug behavior and addiction develop over time – certain substances become more interesting and attractive or simply more practical, take higher priorities, become focal points. And while you're chasing and being chased, things can start to get confusing.

The point is that my drug use was more of a matter of assistance – it was not my focus, my main purpose, my drive, my life. The drugs were not the machine itself, they merely helped the machine run more smoothly, like expensive engine oil for a car. Or something to that effect.

Madness and addiction can prove to be the most natural and tremendous and disastrous of couples, at once beautiful and terrifying. The two work brilliantly in tandem, assisting the willing subject in his or her spiritual ascent and psychological descent.

Even after six years of being clean, not one day seems to pass without my mind tripping over flashes of narco-centric desires – the most torturous of nostalgias. Like tissues scarred for life, scabs that will never heal completely, souvenirs of the most powerful and beautiful thing on earth, each day I am reminded of her warm, welcoming embrace. Hers is an irresistible invitation, a powerful, debilitating temptation...

Every day I awake to the thought of another hit; sometimes it hits me a dozen times a day, more. Even the most fleeting consideration can overpower my mind's ability to entertain any other ideas...she becomes the center of focus, commanding all of my psychic energies, with the evil intention of seducing me to return to the comfort of her welcoming arms. Her embrace appeals incredibly enticing.

But for some reason, I haven't yet. I don't know why. I imagine that some day I may return. I would like to, I expect to - eventually. But for over two years, I've resisted her entreaties and steered clear of her reach. Money, prison, health – these do not enter any rationale for my staying clean. Perhaps I'm afraid of the world to which I would return. Afraid of home, you might say. But which is which? Where do I belong? Here, in your world, in this dullness, in this whiteness? This white room seems expansive, sure, but every direction leads to a white wall. So the question remains: Shall I pass through the roof or pass through the floor?

And in the end, what does it matter?

I succumb to a paralysis.

▪▪▪

i don't bruise easily,
but i bruise often.

and when i do,
the bruises linger long.

i think i have
a natural resistance

to
llllllllllllllllllllllllllllllllllllllllllllllllllllllllllllllllllllllllllllllllllllllllllll
llllllllllllllllllllllllllllllllllllllllllllllllllllllllllllllllllllllllllllllllllllllllllll
ldl

it's like my body,
upon impact,
says no no no;
then once it can say no
no more –

to the hit,
to the strike,
to the contact,
to the blow,

my body
is forced
to acknowledge
the pain,
to acknowledge
that something
physically
happened,
and i can't
deny it,
no matter how much
little
i notice it.

i must recognize
it,
there i have
it,
there it is.

and days later,

it always takes a few days to show,
days later it shows,
and it lingers
long.

and i wake up and see
or i bathe and notice
or i see and realize

that i have this ugly fucking bruise
the size of a grapefruit
on my inner thigh?
my hip? my arm?

why?

i have no idea
where they come from.

■■

When you kick, all the pain comes back. All the pain you had to
kill. All the pain you had tried to kill. It all comes back. I won't
go through that again.

     Junkies don't remember shit. They don't want to. That's
part of it. Think about misery and think about pain. The mental
transcends the physical, and vice versa, simultaneously
consuming, additive. This is something else. One melts into one.
Time is never. This is the goal. To never.

     Just try to think about what it'd be like to be in pain every
moment of your life. Maybe you can't fully understand the whys.
That's part of it too. Why you have or you haven't; why you are
or you aren't.

     If you don't deal with your pain – which is what that shit
allows – you're refusing to fully understand it. You're living
falsely. You're refusing your body its natural way of coping.
Coping with life. This is the ideal – to block off the reality of life,
of pain. You're denying the understanding to ever occur. That's

the point. That's why when you finally kick, you're not just
kicking the habit. You're forced to face all that neglected pain
that you've been denying and refusing, that's been building up.
And, ultimately, you still have to deal with it. Because you never
did, because it's still there.

▪▪▪

Came into work a little late today. Horribly sick. Poisoned. So
bad that I'm considering not drinking for a while.

    I fell over twice this morning. Once when I got out of bed
– I stood up and collapsed in mid-step, falling sideways to the
ground as if struck by an invisible flying wall. Then again – I
tripped on the edge of the tub getting in to take a shower: my left
foot hit the lip and I fell forward, barely breaking my fall with
clumsy blind outstretched hands. Body up against the wall, I sank
to the floor of the tub, water raining down from the sky upon my
hair and body.

    My back hurt. My neck hurt. My head hurt.

    I sucked up the water on my lips onto my tongue and
around the inside of my mouth to moisten that arid cavern
vacuum.

    I was damaged.

    Luckily, I had a training course at work, most of the day
long. "Luckily," because I was incapable of doing any real work.
My vision was shot to hell – all gritty, visibly invisible, blurry and
fuzzy and spotty, everything locomoting by me and before me in
vibrating twists and spirals around and within themselves.

    I felt like I was dying. I guess I was dying. The other
employees in the room – there were about eight of us taking the
course, I think – and the instructor must have thought...

    My body convulsed sporadically as if trying to physically
eject the poison inside me. I shifted in my seat every three
seconds in a futile attempt to locate the nonexistent perfect
position in which I might be comfortable. I'd be hot as hell and
sweating one moment, then cold and shivering the next. I'd put
my sweater on to take it off again.

And then it hit me: the one thing that could take my pain away... I thought of it again, I thought of the way to feel no pain. This thought, this fleeting notion, seized hold of my mind right then and there as I sat in that hard chair, back aching, head hurting, stomach rioting, heart chasing, staring at the computer screen, unable to follow the lesson, deaf to the voice of the trainer, watching his lips move indistinguishably and his eyes dart strange disapprovals at me – at me sitting in that chair, shaking, suffering, paining, and then getting up and running out of the room in the middle of the lecture to barely make it to the bathroom in time to vomit, vomit, vomit, vomit again. My throat burning hell and my eyes bloodshot and watery, I washed my hands and my face and rinsed my mouth out with water.

I'm never drinking again, I said to myself. I looked in the mirror and laughed a nasty look.

■■■

I remember the other day on the subway, I was listening to an older couple speaking in a language that I could not understand. I thought for a long time about what language they were using, and I simply couldn't figure it out.

Now, I'm no linguistics genius, but I'm usually pretty good at this. But I just couldn't identify their tongue for the life of me. I listened again more closely, only catching parts of their utterances for the white noise of the other passengers and the train. I finally gave up, declaring to myself that they were, in fact, speaking a totally made-up language. This thought made me burst into hysterical laughter, at which point even more people stared at me.

■■■

when i blink
and open my eyes,
everything rises.

■■■

Gradually, over the course of the day, my health restored itself. I feel a little better now. I have a couple hours left before I can leave. The training session ended just after five. I don't feel like vomiting anymore.

However, when I got back to my desk after the workshop, my boss came over and said, "Hold off on all other projects and immediately begin working on this highly important urgent matter." Or something to that effect. She stood in front of me for the next fifteen minutes iterating the importance of this task and the procedure I must follow and stressing the part that I absolutely must finish by the end of the business day tomorrow.

But I couldn't understand a word she said, as all of a sudden I was forced to command all my focus and energy on not vomiting all over her.

Then she left, and now I'm stuck with this "highly important urgent matter," but no clue as to what I'm expected to do. Fortunately, it's due tomorrow. I will wait until the morning, to approach the project with a clear mind.

This was after my second shit of the day. I went and took another, and now, as I said, I feel a little better.

■ ■

I remember a dream from last night:

I'm sitting with my shrink in his office.

"How are your ribs doing?" he asks.

"They're fine," I say, noticing that they hurt.

"Do you want some sauce?" he asks. I thank him, declining the offer, and take a bite. Juicy. The couple in the corner leaves the room. He reaches down into a desk drawer, pulling out a bottle of pills and handing them to me. "Try these. They're delicious."

I take the bottle from his hands. All moves slowly. I turn the tiny plastic container around between my fingers and read the label: hydromorphone. Immediately overjoyed, I rip off the cap; then, thinking I should, I say: "What kind of a doctor are you?"

He mumbles something, I can't remember. Something about him understanding, I'm sure. Makes sense to me. He picks at a red stain on his apron.

"Mind if I....?"

"Go right ahead," he says, reaching back into his desk drawer and handing me a pen. I don't remember cooking it up but the next thing I know the stopper's pushed in.

...the shit hits me...

...it is indeed very therapeutic...

He is a good doctor, I think to myself, smiling, warm, floating, cuddled.

The amazing thing about dreamworld is how real sensations can be. I got high. I felt it, like it was real. It felt great, really real. Just like I remember it...

"You want..." I ask carelessly, barely able to articulate, my flushed cheeks frozen soft. He shakes his head, No, then brings out some cocaine. He cuts some aside and blasts an impressive line. He looks up at me and smiles. I attempt to reach over, to somehow signal to him to allow me a bit. But I find myself rendered immobile, my body like a mass of iron jelly. I sit in the chair and sit. The brilliant opaque cloud of numbnessness and euphoria descends upon me and envelopes me in its soft billowy blanket of warm weathered silk.

■■

It is six thirty now and I can go home soon enough. I have promised myself not to drink at all tonight or tomorrow. Then it'll be Friday, and I can allow myself to get drunk on the weekend.

But I should cut down on my drinking, especially during the week. It causes me too much pain. I have come to terms with pain as a quintessential, inextricable part of my existence. But enough is enough.

Part of my plan is to smoke more marijuana. Another way I cloud keep my drinking down is by scoring... This seems like the perfect solution. I wouldn't have to drink as much, and I wouldn't have to eat as much, and I wouldn't have to shit as much. I could make it through life never feeling pain again – just constant euphoria, constantly.

This is a great idea. I always wanted to be a junkie. It's a shame it didn't work out before. But it can work. I'll make it work. Watch me.

I feel better already, filled with hope.

The junkie's dream: to rise above.

■■

my brain
is like a fish;
it swims
and has gills.

■■

If it wasn't for all the crazies, I wouldn't enjoy living in the city as much as I do.

They add a lot of life to this faux-lively place, amidst these people who subsist as half-drained batteries, scorched lightning rods, antidotes, anyway.

But without the crazies, I might feel self-conscious about myself in public; because of them, I can freely talk to myself. I can sing, drink, whatever passes my fancy, without attracting too much attention.

■■

Yesterday, I was quite sure I was going to die. Alcohol poisoning is no joke. I can't believe that I made it through the entire day at work. And even if I wasn't going to die, which I didn't, then I was most definitely in the process of dying. But I guess we always are, are we not?

But today is another day – and, alas, I am still here, with my problems and my pains. Of course, I picked up a fifth of whiskey last night on my way home from work. So there's that.

My stomach speaks. I have to go to the bathroom.

Anyway, I accomplished absolutely nothing today. Maybe that's why the day seemed so long. Time goes by quicker if you're somehow kept occupied. And if you're not kept busy, with one thing or another, your mind may begin working on its own...

But that's not what I sat down to write about...

Oh yes – I spent the entire work day staring at this enormous mound of paper on my desk, flipping through this two thousand one hundred forty three page report and typing a bit and all in all miserably failing to figure out what the piss I was supposed to be doing with it, to it, for it, at it, whatever. This is the project my boss gave me yesterday when I was sick.

Then, around two o'clock, six hours having pissed and me approaching the two thousands and still having no clue about any of it, my eyes left feeling permanently out of focus, my mouth dry, my head light and heavy, I got up from my desk, zombied down the hallway, and knocked on my boss' door.

When she answered and invited me to enter, I did not sit down but instead simply asked her if she could come over to my desk as "I seem to be a tad bit confused about this one aspect of the report..."

She obliged, followed me to my desk, and spent the next half hour flipping through the papers. Taking the cue, I proceeded to flip through some random papers on my desk, successfully (I think) achieving the appearance of actually doing something. I furrowed my brow at certain moments. I defocused my eyes for fun, making the words on the page swell blurry.

After what seemed like nineteen hours, she leaned over and began to babble indecipherably... I struggled desperately trying to comprehend her abstract vocal emissions, to decipher some actual words and meaningful phrases, to latch onto something (you may have noticed that this is a recurring problem of mine, but this time I believe my incomprehension owed more to her unintelligible staggered stuttered mutterings than to my own shattered consciousness).

At some point I began to formulate some sense out of her nonsensical utterances... – but luckily I didn't have to be sure about anything, as my boss suddenly straightened up, "You know what," she said, "this might be more complicated than I thought...I don't know where...hgmmm...yeh, you see... – well, these results need to be updated... Just drop this off at my desk, please – I need to take a look at this before I give it back to you..."

I wondered briefly why she couldn't take the report to her desk herself, but instead I smiled a crescent moon and she laughed, "Don't get too excited." She smiled, and I smiled some more.

I smiled because I did absolutely nothing of value today.

This day, August 17th, will forever remain the day that passed without me.

- -

I have to finish this whole bottle of water before I call it a night. It's Saturday. It's already almost midnight and I've been drinking since noon and I'm not trying to drink so much today but I'm not tired yet and I gotta do something.

- -

I recently learned the stupidity of the expression, "Free as a bird."

I spent some time watching birds in the park the other day.

As far as I can tell, they just poke at the ground and shit all over the place. This does not appeal to me as an enviable mode of existence. I agree that it would be nice to be able to fly, but I think that, at the end of the day, I would find hands and arms, not wings, more suitable to my lifestyle.

I was looking at pigeons, though. Maybe other birds have it better.

- -

i'm once again reaching
a point in my life
in i become aware
that i am totally unawares.

days go by

without me real
i
zing them;

i find
half empty
drinks
everywhere.

scattered mind
and body aching;
i'm tired
and i've been tired for days.

this seems to happen
regularly
though
on average only
several times
the year.

and these are the days
drink in hand
that
pour into each other
until
i can't
anymore.

and what will happen is that
i'll tone it down
a notch
only to later
bring it up again.

scattered mind,
body aching,

half empty drinks.

one of these days,
i'll tell you about yesterday.

until then,
i drink to another tomorrow.

■■

Just walked into the office and already they're gabbing away, one
of the secretaries spitting some craziness about waking up at three
thirty in the morning, *as usual.*
        As usual?
        As usual, I feel like shit.
        I wonder if this woman is capable of realizing just how
much she talks.
        She talks a great fucking deal.
        It probably wouldn't aggravate me so much if we weren't
next-cubicle neighbors. But we are, and because of the proven
weakness of the gray partition space division wall (not a real wall
– not my friend), I can hear every word she says.
        Her phone conversations last at least fifteen minutes – the
fifteen minute ones being those with people she's never met
before, like a plumber or landscaper or pizza delivery person. Or
whatever. Total fucking strangers and she won't shut her mouth,
can't stop talking. Really, it's like a disease. I know more about
her than I know about myself. Maybe that's a bad example.

■■

My problem with reality is that I do not care about it. At all. It's
that simple.
        Though you may find this to be in contradiction with my
anxious deliberations over the meaning(lessness) of my life.

■■

I'm going to let you in on a little secret: there's nothing in my briefcase, like my rectum.

It's true. I keep nothing in there.

Nevertheless, nearly every five out of seven days for the last two years I have carried this brown leather case with me to and from work, as if the object and the act sufficiently confirm my professionalism.

Sometimes I wonder what the others put in their briefcases, and if the contents are actually of any value or ever utilized. I imagine brown paper bags with sandwiches and small plastic bags with carrots. Next to some folders and papers, right? I imagine that some people take their work home with them?

I don't know. I try not to wonder long about this.

∎∎∎

Sudden spontaneous bursts of immense anger and frustration, squeezing seizing overwhelming yet I must conquer and suppress, though always I remain clouded, possessed with a lingering urge to bite off the flesh of IS and spit IS out, mangled disfigured mutilated mauled.

∎∎∎

I stay up all night drinking, waiting for nothing to happen. I don't know why I can't just go to sleep.

But I can't sleep. I don't have the urge to sleep. I only want to keep drinking and smoking. That is all.

So I will sit here and do this and do this until I can no longer do this.

I pour a near-full glass of scotch, cut it with a splash of water, put it up to my lips, and throw it down.

I rest my forehead against my forearm across my desk.

I look sideways at the bottle.

I think to myself, What am I killing here?

Myself, I answer, knowingly.

∎∎∎

I'm getting a bit jumpy these days. Jittery. Uneasy.

The blood inside my veins inside my body acts distressed.

They say that physical exercise can assuage and diminish mental anxiety. "They" includes my psychiatrist.

So I thought I'd give it a shot, to try to feel a little healthier, to try to calm my nerves. I decided to try swimming, having located some idea that I possessed the ability to.

I picked a gym conveniently situated near my workplace, optimistically considering the possibility of getting into the habit of swimming regularly after work.

First, I had to sign up for a membership and pay an exorbitant annual fee. And I had to endure such miserable bureaucracy in the form of filling out forms. They even scanned my barcode – in front of other people, no less!

When I had finally passed all of their tests, changed into my swimming trunks in the locker room, rinsed off as prescribed, walked to the pool area and jumped in the water, a nightmare of the flesh awaited me.

After a few pleasant laps, a vision so malicious and insidious presented itself to me, corrupting any sense of relaxation I may have achieved up until that point, casting me into the dark abyss of agony: I saw, demonically skimming the surface, curling across the top of the water like an ever-extending web of sinuous smoke, the figure of a barely visible serpent heading directly at me with an incontrovertible air of crazed hunger in its bright red eyes.

With never-before-realized adeptness (born of pure, abject fear), I instinctively dove under the approaching sea monster, swam frantically beneath it to the nearest edge of the pool, and madly jumped out of the perilous waters.

On my feet again, on land, my heart raced as I gasped for air; I wiped my wet face with my wet hands and stared fearfully at the water where I had just been swimming. I repeatedly and near-violently stroked my back with the knuckles and thumb of my right hand, overcome with the disturbing sensation of having literally brushed up against the evil water dragon.

I knew that the beast was hiding now, invisible, but I knew better than to get back in the water. Shaken, attempting to regain my composure and a regularized heartbeat, pitying the fools who were unaware of the danger they faced – but sensible enough not to draw attention to myself by screaming in panic – I made my way to the locker room as collectedly as I could manage.

I calmed down in the sauna. My breathing slowed to a deliberate, deep, clear nasal draw. The heat warmed my blood, slowed me down, and I enjoyed the ease of the sensation of calmly and totally perspiring.

When I was showered and dressed and ready to leave the locker room, I could not find the exit.

No door was marked, and I found myself pacing back and forth in what became a compartmentalized labyrinth for overgrown rats. My exasperation grew to an intolerable level until finally a group of men appeared and I uncontrollably blurted out, "How the fuck do you get out of this place?"

They laughed, though thankfully not in a persecuting manner, and one of them pointed to an unmarked door. I laughed too, to cover myself, and then exited.

There is nowhere safe for me to go. I shall never return to that cell. This is what I get for listening to the advice of others.

■■■

one week
one weak
i read a sign
one of those church signs:

      "seven days without prayer
      makes one weak."

i read that sign
on my way home
from the subway
to my apartment

and i laughed
like a madman

all the way to my door.

▪▪

Now what am I going to write.

I need to try to make this section more coherent and sober than the first part.

This section of *New Roses*, to be entitled *the Flowers Bloom*, should start with an admission of purpose in words – maybe an acknowledgment of failure: "I was going to," no, "My original intention in this, the second and final section of *New Roses*, was to tell you of the wonderful ways in which my life has changed for the better, to illustrate to you how much I've grown over the years, to convey how it is possible for one to learn from his mistakes, to relate to you the fact that I am a new person with a newfound comfort and understanding of self and place."

That'd be great.

Unfortunately, I am unable to convince myself that I'm better off now than I was before. This is important. When I look back at the person that I imagine to be the one who wrote *the Truth*, and the person that I feel is the one who is writing *the Flowers Bloom*, I couldn't pick one's existence as preferable over the other.

People only change a bit at a time. Most people never change at all. I've had lengthy discussions on this topic with some doctors I've known, and I maintain that people never really change, they just find new ways of expressing themselves. Oftentimes the people who appear to have changed most drastically are really only finally revealing that which had always been inside them. That or they're newly denying themselves part of themselves.

But the second section should also...make some statement about the difficulty in conveying anything, let alone an entire decade of a man's life...like, what should I tell you? What should I include, what do I merely touch upon, what do I omit entirely?

Maybe what's of most importance is my conscious and/or unconscious reconstruction (meaning, necessarily, reduction) of my past. All histories involve elision; hence, that which I choose not to write (and the process of arriving at that decision) can be as (if not more) significant as that which I do write, narratively and psychologically, as an indication of what I find to be important and unimportant in my life.

But since you don't know what I'm not telling you, you would have a hard time assessing the significance of the methodology of my selectivity.

■■■

The eyes have again begun to weigh heavily upon me, and I wonder why they've decided upon returning. I find it rude and offensive, undoubtedly malicious in intent.

I sense Death approaching. I recognize this feeling very really, as we have encountered each other before.

■■■

I have no appetite. No interest in food. Historically, personally, this is nothing new.

I feel like I'm withering away. I've lost a lot of weight. I like the idea of there being physically less of me. I think about slowly starving myself to death. To gradually decrease until I die. And then what's left of my body will decompose, leaving a skeleton of a man that has no meaning...until my bones completely disintegrate and become one with the soil – and nothing will remain of my physical existence.

A beautiful thought, if I may say so myself! How exciting – how goddamn exhilarating! I breathe triumphantly, now as I will not then...

■■■

This morning, as I was standing on the subway platform waiting for the train, I thought (I always imagine someone coming up behind me and pushing me onto the tracks just as the train is coming in, and I think about dying that way, of being plowed over by the oncoming stampede of subway cars – which is what I was thinking when this other thought occurred to me) that maybe the reason I did opiates was because I was afraid to die – or, more accurately, because I was afraid to die in pain. And that everything else I embraced and imbibed, maybe it was all to die, to defy death by killing myself, or to defy life by having a clouded consciousness, so that life would not be life, and that death would not be death. Just a thought.

. . . .

But I haven't killed myself yet. You know why?
     I'll tell you:
     No reason.
     Ha!
     I hope that made you uncomfortable.
     Whatever.
     The truth is, I have no reason to live, so, therefore, logically, I have no reason to die.
     What would my suicide note read?
     I was bored.
     That's weak.
     No reason is not a reason.
     Plus it's not worth it. I'm going to die soon enough anyway – of this I am sure. My life has been egregiously unhealthy. I have harmed myself in so many ways, as often as possible, to the extreme. My body simply cannot handle much more. And if I'm going to die soon, why rush it? Well, I already have, you're right. But I see no point in taking my death myself.
     More importantly, though, I am now absolutely certain that they are going to kill me. They will kill me, I know, unless I die first, which is unlikely, considering their tradition of meticulousness in operation.
     But the thought that has always fucked me up is that taking my own life is the only way to affirm free will. This is not a novel idea, but its validity always kicks my ass mentally. I didn't choose this life – but I can choose my death. (Perhaps.) It's the

only way for a human being to fully realize his or her existence –
by exercising the conscious ability to end it.

Then again, if something's going to happen, then it will
happen – what's the sense of interfering with the natural Time of
the Clock?

Unless, of course, the mechanism requires the interference
or participation of an outside force – then...ah, shit. I don't know.
This is what my trapeze does all fucking day while I sit and stare
at this goddamn computer screen and lose my eyes in a plane that
is no deeper than it is. Because if this river's course is fixed, then
how can we be sure of ourselves, and since we can never realize
the river's direction or its final destination until the very moment
we arrive at the present, the ultimate absurdity resides in our
attempts at blindly yet so boldly navigating the flow. And if we
impose our own direction and destination, it wouldn't matter at
all, either way, fixed or not fixed, for we are always exactly there,
wherever we are when we are there, until the moment we are no
longer there but somewhere else, at which point we are still
exactly at that place and time.

And, until then, I am still here.

■■

I'm trying to battle these demons and I just fucking hate myself. I
drink too much and I know it's killing me but I can't fucking stop.

I'm usually okay but it's after five or six days straight
getting wasted that really fucking kills me. My body and my
mind.

My nerves are completely shot and I can't seem to silence
the voices – they're becoming more pronounced – louder, more
incessant – more powerful, more commanding. All I want is for
them to stop, to shut up.

But they persist in torturing me. I refuse to give their
voices space here.

My body, my skin, my gin-soaked blood, my throat, my
stomach, my intestines – it's all fucked.

Shaky and raw.

I suffer every way, either way, every fucking day.

But I like to drink.

....

since i learned
how to see
i have watched myself
wither away

....

I went to the bar last night. I didn't see him at first but he arrived
after a few beers. We chatted for a while to get natural and
comfortable. Then he slipped me a dose under a corner of the
napkin under my beer.

What thoughts just then raced through my mind I trembled
handing him the money beneath the bar in anticipation smiling
nervous and impulsively full of hope rush. I felt like I felt the first
time I ever bought this shit, anxious and excited and scared – but
this time was different, of course, because I knew what to expect.
This is the second first time, and it will be tremendous, I thought
to myself. And before I knew it, my friend had disappeared as if
he had never been there and I found myself sitting at the bar alone
again.

I picked up my beer, my left hand reaching over and
carefully crumpling up the dope-napkin and sliding it into my
pocket. The bartender, whom I've come to consider a friend,
looked at me a little suspiciously, reservedly judgmental, as he
pulled a pint for someone.

My beer was empty. Not wanting to fulfill my bartender-
friend's expectations by getting up and leaving – confirming my
guilt in such a reproachable act: transaction completed, having
come to the bar only to buy drugs, time to leave and get high – I
motioned for another beer. I did not want him to think less of me.

The junk that I had surreptitiously slipped into my pants
pocket reigned supreme over my mind. I put my hand in my
pocket and separated the goods from the napkin; I felt it, fingering
it between the tips of my index and middle fingers. My heart

raced. I slowly took my hand out of my pocket as the bartender brought me my beer. I nodded and put some money down.

"I got your tab going," looking down at me.

"Right yes, of course," I smiled stupidly. What did he think of this unwonted aberration? I never paid per drink – I always settled with him at the end. It must be obvious, my strange behavior. What was he thinking? Did he know? Had I just confirmed my guilt? He turned around with not another word about the matter.

I thought about getting up and going to the bathroom...I had pocketed a straw earlier...just in case...but no, I shouldn't...not here.

But. All I could think about was the shit in my pocket and getting it back into my body where I wanted it, where it belonged, for the shit to course through my veins and I am made of shit blood yes god. My beer vanished in two minutes. I ordered another one. I wanted to get out of that bar and get home and get great, get really really fucking great. My beer was gone again and I ordered another. I wasn't going to let him think anything like that of me. I have control. I'm not a junkie.

It was on my mind, on my mind, on my mind, until:

"What?" I found myself stirred, awaken.

"Last call, man," he said.

Oh shit. I looked around an empty bar...

I settled my tab and thanked the man. We shook hands good-bye; I turned and exited the room gracelessly.

■ ■

Drunk as I was, I barely got any sleep last night. Somehow I managed the strength to leave the shit for a better time, to not use it – to not *waste* it – dead drunk. I fell out quickly but slept very poorly – half dazed, half crazed, my thoughts and my dreams blending in and out, rendered indistinguishable, as I passed in and out of sleep...

And now I'm at work, exhausted and wide awake, anxiously anticipating the special treat that is waiting for me at home.

■ ■

i remember
sitting on the floor
of the kitchen,
naked,
pressing a knife
hard
against
my flesh,
drawing
the blade
across
my arm,

to slice my skin,
to tattoo my skin,
to draw out the in,
to feel a physical pain,
to balance out
the pain within.

      i know
      a lot of people
      think:

      i don't know what
      would ever possess
      someone to do
      something like that.

i wanted blood, baby.

■ ■

I will take the time now to explain that my use of the word "I"
signifies another person.

I am not referring to the "I", "i", and "Ii"s of *the Truth* – that's another story, with its own significations.

Throughout this section, when I use the word "I", I only mean one person – the "I" who lives in the world (your world – the "real world"). This section has only one narrator, and a narrator concerned with only one character-self at that.

There exists the man who lives and the man who writes. Both units constitute *myself* as it is conventionally understood *only as one*. But this is my world here, so I can be honest about it.

What this means is that my autobiographical presentation is twice removed: first, my one self experiences (relates to his consciousness), who then relates it to me (the writer who relates it to you). This is to say nothing of the others involved.

Therefore, you must recognize that I am a fraud, an imposter, and not to be trusted. Because I am subjectively interpreting that which an other has already subjectively interpreted – even if these selves occur within the same corporeal shell.

■■■

It's been over a month since I last sat down to write. The workplace is driving me mad. I've decided that I must stop this torture; so, I put in my two weeks' notice a few days ago. I can't do this shit anymore, it doesn't mean anything to me. I just can't do it.

These people...they have no idea who I am, where I've been, what I've done. It's all a fucking farce. I'm perpetuating this farce. It's disgusting.

And these people think to know me – though they really are incapable. For they have never experienced the gird of mental abandon, its appeals and its dangers, the freedom and the pain, a silence quieter than seven swallows' moons battling against the deafening screech of the sirens that reel from the rapids-rolling rocks in the rivers of the psyche, the undeniable pleasantries of addiction and aggravated psychosis. The euphoria of madness.

No, they cannot recognize the defeated eyes of a junkie, a felon, a lunatic. They have never been on the inside. They live on the outside. They deny the inside. And so it remains at polite smiles and handshakes. What is there to say to these People?

For the pupils of submission are distinctive and betray the truth to those who have seen – the truth of the past, of the experience of light, of the distracting desires, of my strongest desires, my incessant unchanging thoughts about the one true thing in this winner's world of liars and cheaters, the only truth ever to be found amidst the debris and pre-wreckage of the human soul, the unholy sanctuary of the disparate desperate demons of freedom...

They do not know, and I stay quiet and say nothing. One must first see the chains to be able to remove them.

I feel my return, and I can only embrace my self.

And so, with these thoughts, I have resigned my post at the office.

The reason that I have returned to writing after this month lapse is truly profound and shocking; I will now attempt to explain it, although one must understand that mere words only corrupt and dishonor my intent, that human words will always fail to fully convey the naked truth of the reality of experience:

Last weekend, I found myself detachedly strolling through a borough that I rarely visit.

(Oftentimes I take such walks, reflexively almost, in the evening after work or during the afternoons on my days off. It is a habit of mine that I developed after moving to the city. Sometimes I find myself in an unfamiliar neighborhood, several miles from my apartment, and I look at the Time and realize that I've been out walking for hours. These walks afford me a calm that I find difficult to achieve otherwise. It is an exercise in removing my self from my body, and it takes Time: I pass from an acknowledgment of being to an understanding of not being, the transition from consciously walking to unconsciously walking and purely thinking. Spending such time with my self allows me to isolate my self, to remove me from me. I enter into external existence, I pass through to the outside of my body. I feel like an amoeba and think like nothing.)

And so, peaceful and unconsciously meandering, I turned one fateful corner, whereupon the light in the back of my head flickered. I felt an accompanying change in atmosphere: the cool November air tightened up and cracked itself open – a gesture of acceptance. I slowed down a bit but continued walking, alert, hearing nothing but the eerily amplified ambient echo of my shoes repeatedly hitting the ground.

No winds blew, no persons passed by, no cars drove past, no birds scuttled around at my feet, no rats slinked along the gutter, and no distant sirens wailed. Movement and action and sound and all the other aspects of the mechanism had come to a halt – in order to permit this total suspension of Time. All had seemingly agreed to suspend itself and I knew that it was in order to communicate something to me.

So I stopped, and listened carefully, expecting to hear something.

I stood there, waiting, in the center of a sidewalk square.

And then I realized that it had nothing to do with sound – and with simultaneous dread and delight, I got it: I was standing on the street from my visions. I was there. It existed. It was real.

It was absolutely uncanny – a perfect reconstruction of the setting of the scene of my death as played again and again in my mind, the exact block I've envisioned my stabbing so many times over the past several years. I knew this location better than anywhere, better than any place I'd ever been before. It was amazing.

"So this is it," I said to myself, "this is the fucking place. It is real, after all."

I then saw the man approaching me in my mind – but it was not to be. A cloud moved above, as only clouds can when all is frozen, obfuscating the light of the sun and casting a thick cloak of darkness over the street. I glanced skyward and knew that the sun was hiding for a reason.

"So, not today, huh?" I addressed the sun through the cloud. "Well, when then?" I awaited a response, though none arrived. "What do I do now? Now that I know? What do they expect from me? Can you tell me? Please?"

No answer. My eyes and my mind returned to the earth to notice that the street was now bustling with city life, pedestrians everywhere...and also, luckily, just in time to notice two uniformed policemen making their way down the sidewalk towards me, accompanied by a dog and its old lady, the crotchety grandma leading the way, pointing at me and shouting accusatorily.

It seemed like the right time to resume my stroll.

I turned the corner and hustled into the first bar I could find. I ordered two whiskeys and two beers for the both of us, and nestled down in the corner to think this over with myself.

■■■

I realized – before it was too late! – that I had been ignoring the ticking of a bomb, a ticking within that I had been deafly tasting the entire time, mutely hearing, blindly feeling – and then all of a sudden, having regained my nose, I realized the encroaching danger pursuing me. I began calculating the ticks against the seconds and it was close and it became closer and it just kept getting closer and closer and I had no idea when this thing would blow and I realized that NOW IS THE TIME to leave or else there would be nothing left of me to save. And so again, thus, it became clear to me that the Time to quit my job had arrived.

■■■

But for making it at this office for nearly two whole years, I'm pretty impressed with myself. I should have quit after my first paycheck. But no! No, I persevered, numbing myself to the bored drumming of the drone of the drumming of the drones.

■■■

Now that my convictions have been verified, I must not betray the slightest sense of fear. On the contrary, I must show them that not only am I fully aware of their plans, but that I am not afraid. In fact, I will behave in just the opposite manner expected and boast my discovery fearlessly, confidently: I intend to visit the block as often as possible, as a sort of ritual acknowledgment and acceptance.

My revelation must be treated with the greatest seriousness and care, without distraction or interference. I need to appropriately devote my time and my mind to this new chapter of my life, likely the last chapter of my life, my death.

■■

Here, for example, the birds.

■■

I have so many scars over my hands and arms...elsewhere, too. Nothing serious – I've never been in a war between nations.

I regard my scars as mementos of sorts, souvenirs left by tough women and hard nights of self-abuse – even though for the most part, the origins of these scars escape me.

Whenever I notice these dark, toughened spots of skin, I slowly trace them with my fingers and think of knives, broken glass, nails. I cannot help but regard them fondly, as something I created, or else something that has otherways become an inextricable part of me. This is my body, whether I like it or not.

■■

on my way to work,
i saw a blind man
walking
down the street.

he looked at me
and smiled.

■■

I can't say that I have any regrets in regards to wasting these two years or so working this job – it's more of a lackadaisical sigh, an, Oh well, what can I do about it now? Nothing. Except maybe learn from my mistakes? Have I been true to myself, whatever that may mean? Have I been true? I believed...I certainly believed...but...I am delusional...I feel nauseated...

Yet happy with the fact that I've only two more days to worry this miserable job.

━━━

I read somewhere that the word 'paranoid' means 'to see around things.' I like this.

━━━

For the past two weeks, I've been making regular pilgrimages (at least three times a week) to the block where I will be killed. As soon as I no longer have to work, I will visit the place of my death every day, until the day that they make their move, the day that will be my final day. My act must be understood as an assertion of confidence, of fearlessness.

I am ready.

━━━

I don't think I mentioned that I stopped taking my medications a week ago. It may have been more than a week ago now. It may have been two weeks ago – perhaps even longer.

I stopped taking them because I wanted to remember how I feel, naturally, without medical/chemical/pharmaceutical influence.

And now I can tell you: naturally, I feel terrible.

The skin around my cranium feels like it's filled with a thick heavy gel fluid. I feel cracks in my skull and I expect my head to explode into a million green onion caviar sperm shit blood puss coil worms at any second.

My chest feels very far away though my heart beats faster than a hummingbird's wings. My head and my body seem to pull away from each other in revulsion like two negatively charged magnetic fields.

Why do I always have to think about how I feel, what I think? Why can't I simply be? Exist normally, at peace? I don't know if there can be a normality of existence – I just don't want to constantly stress about being stressed. What am I doing, where am I, what am I doing here, what is happening about me, why is this the way this is? Why is?

I I wan't to relax and breathe easy, work and freely play without the burdensome anxiety of endless analysis it shouldn't be this difficult to breathe right. Some weeks have passed since I got high that second first time. I have been exercising restraint, with some difficulty. But, the wait is over; today I got high again. I will soon, again, and more.

▪▪

Today is another day, except that it is not like any other – for it is my last day at work!

And so here I sit, at my desk, impatiently as mindlessly whiling away the hours with the conviction parallel only to that of an apathetic drone. You know this part already. But I feeleeleel goode.

The tiny clock on my computer screen when I drag the mouse pointer thing down to the bottom of the screen corner reads four colon forty seven. I have until six colon fifteen until I can leave.

In retrospect (as I consider instead of work):

the past few years of my life of my life have been the most socially acceptable and exemplary years of my life. Concomitantly, they have also been the most worthless and least productive in terms of my market value personal worthiness-o-meter of mescaline metamorphosed mercury. I've made day I've made money and I've made little else. The past two years or so at this job have been a repetitive route of continuous repetitious routine every day is the same every day is the same every day is the wake up, too sick to breakfast, too sick to choke cigarette, I shower, try to shave without cutting myself, try to shave and not cut myself, make it to work ten minutes late no matter what time I wake up and make it out of the apartment always ten minutes late.

Work for the next nine hours, take a half hour break for lunch as opposed to the encouraged one hour break for lunch or just skip lunch entirely and take a ten to smoke. The ladies talk too much, the men not enough (though still too much). My boss is nice but has a look in her eyes that could easily be described as satanic from the audience's perspective in that great big theatre where I took my seat next to the harlot's slaves where we all sit still and same and stare at the big screen spectacle all day and view, review, revise, proofread, edit, enter data, scan, print.

Most of my Time at work, here over the past nearly two years, I spent staring empty blank at the big computer screen before me in dolorous ineptitude. The rest of the Time I spent writing this garbage as I'm doing now.

Then at the end of the work day I would leave for home, usually around seven. At my apartment, I'd try to eat dinner, which worked about seventy-five percent of the time. Wasted from work, I'd quickly get wasted on booze, whereupon I would work on the booze until I successfully passed out. But as I lay me down to sleep, I could never chase away the desire to never go to work again, to never get out of bed, to never wake up again. To never.

And yet, the next morning, I'd wake up, hungover as the morning last, and arrive at work ten minutes late. Always the same, always with nothing to differentiate between one day and the next and the previous. Every day, and I've been here before. It was crushing me. But after today, the monotonous drudgery ends, and I start anew.

■■

I think of the rats.

■■

My boss and five or six of my closest co-workers took me out for dinner at the end of the day. It was very awkward, and surprisingly emotional for me. In fact, I almost cried – not because I was sad to be leaving the job or the office or the people but because I felt that they actually cared. Their emotions, their sentiments, rubbed off on me; I was sad and almost cried because they were sad and almost crying. As I said, it was awkward.

The restaurant was nice, and the gesture was appreciable, but it was all very difficult for me. Everyone was looking at me, everyone wanted a piece of me to take home with them, they all wanted me to answer their questions. I felt bombarded, overwhelmed. I tried to play it cool, took great efforts in appearing collected; I had always tried to be the person that I thought I should be for them, which became the person that they thought I was – a person I had created for them, for their protection as well as mine, for the sake of professional longevity, just in case. But now that my final day at work had ended, and I would never have to return to those offices or see these people ever again, my energy and my attitude toward them had changed. I no longer had to act, to perform for them; I had nothing to lose. I felt changed; I felt distant. The individuals seated with me at the table, my coworkers, people with whom I had worked closely for the past two years, with whom I had established personal relationships, working and even (somewhat) social, now appeared to me as total strangers. They were supposed to be my friends, but in truth they meant nothing to me at all.

The red lights on the restaurant's ceiling landed blocks of glares shining upon the polished wooden table. The standard motions of restaurant dining were expertly attended to: drinks were refilled, plates removed, silverware replaced, the following course served; my fellow diners performed well, properly engaging in insignificant banter, renewing facial expressions accordingly, extending amicable gestures and polite compliments... It was like I was thrown on stage, in the middle of a play, without a part. And the band played on.

I looked down at the food on my plate. A sudden physical detachment came over me, as if I was watching me, and the entire dinner party, from an outside perspective.

My fork felt cold in my hot hand sweat. The smell of damp cement and steel presented itself. I pushed the dish away the plate screeched so loud against the surface of the table shrieked so loud that I pulled it back right away so as to not draw more attention upon myself.

I persevered to maintain propriety, though I truly felt that I wasn't really there, that it wasn't me they were celebrating but someone else who was occupying my body, that I could do nothing but sit next to me and watch the whole scene.

At least it was dinner, because that meant I could drink. We weren't allowed to drink alcohol during lunch, though of course I always did. The point is I didn't have to hide it. And also, it being dinner with several heads, various dialogues abounded, and I could avoid being the center of attention.

My glass of wine was empty and so I filled it from the bottle of wine that was on the table. Wine. I smiled uncomfortably, glancing around the table at these People. Disease flooded my veins and I downed the wine fast to steady my nerves. My eyes met with the eyes on the faces on the heads on the bodies that surrounded the table, and as no one wore a look of reproach I quietly and steadily refilled my glass. I sipped it more slowly this time. I sat there like that, at that table, occasionally lifting my glass to my lips, as if with no motion at all, pretending to pay attention, seeing my voice answer questions I couldn't hear, pretending not to move at all, pretending to be totally aware and present in the moment, all the while just thinking about breathing, breathing, breathing through my nose, measuredly, slowly, in a tried and forced calm. I ate as much of my meal as I could (not much) and drank as little as possible (a lot).

At the end of the meal, we parted ways, all projecting pleasantries and gratefulness and intentions to keep in touch. I went home in a taxi and got high.

....

I never dealt with it. The fucking shrink was right, and I knew it all along. So I have devised the perfect plan to both deal and not deal, for ever and ever.

Fuck you and your death. I don't need either of them shits. I've had enough of both.

It is about that time when something about that time is to be that time.

■■

Time to reflect, if I can do so coherently.

I have spent the majority of my life struggling with life. I have been diagnosed mentally ill on numerous occasions. I have been medicated for as long as I can remember. I have been institutionalized many times, crowned by three years and seven months of a four and a half year sentence in prison for various criminal offenses. I clearly have difficulty living in your world.

My body carries a perpetual panicked emptiness, my mind is tortured by a near-constant frantic need to fill the void within. The more I pour down my throat or inject into my blood the more complete, the more whole I feel. It makes me feel filled and not empty. But it does make me feel, truly feel. Like cutting myself. It's a warmth that I need. It helps. But it's never enough. Drinking has caused me too much pain. Junk has caused me pain, but the pain washes away with the next hit. The antidote is more venom. The painlessness ends in pain, the pain is painlessnesslessness.

The contradiction of achieving feeling through numbness is a necessary, defining characteristic of my mind's relationship to my body. To conquer. To live freely. To be one, one whole, only one, undivided.

■■

I walk down that street almost every day now. An overpowering, undeniable force commands me there. Now, if I miss my daily visit, I become anxious, overcome by the emptiness of unfulfilled desire. And the next day I return. Always in the afternoon, just before I take my lunch, lunch being the first meal of my day, after noon. In my eyes in my mind I see Death come under a full sun and so it must be around this time that I will be killed, so that the sun can hit the street directly from above. When it rains I sometimes choose not to go, and at these times my break from

ritual does not distress me as much. But most of the time I go
anyway. I want to make sure that they know that I am not afraid.
My habitual visitations constitute a defiant complicity, a
rebellious submission. I don't care about dying. By welcoming
their intention to murder me, I am revealing how little I value their
world. I know that they understand this.

▪▪

what what why

no

i i

no

shrieks like arrows

icy calamities and crumbling buildings and tearing tearing apart
the flesh of the one –

> that unlatched the clasp
> and accepted Time

> for it was never nothingness
> it was ever neverness

> always my ideal to never

and so I go
into the chaos of a different freedom,
unto death...

the blossom of pain,
the flower of truth,
the fruit of life,
the garden of Death,

the end of dream:

> I have made up my mind.
> I will define my Time.

■ ■

I have only one option, as I see it, apart from idly waiting for them to take action. This will constitute the ultimate act of subversion, what will assert my humanity while taking it away, what will put my life into my own hands, my death into my own hands, while still fulfilling my destiny, and while proudly trumping the Ones that have made my life a living hell.

I have decided the following: I will arrange for someone to kill me on that very block, to kill me before they kill me, to kill me exactly according to their intentions, as communicated to me in my visions.

The more I think about foiling their plan to murder me by executing it myself, the more it seems to me to be a wonderful, brilliant idea. When I put myself in their shoes, I imagine how I'd feel if someone did that to me. Think about it: you want to kill someone, but someone else beats you to it – and that person is the very one you wanted to kill! One and the same! How infuriating! I would be pissed if someone pulled that on me. It's perfect – absolutely brilliant!

So I think I'll go through with it. Yeh. I must.

■ ■

Finding someone who is willing to help me should not be difficult. I will very carefully select the contracted killer, and will offer a more than reasonable compensation. Years ago I made up a will that entitled all my earthly possessions to anyone who happened to kill me. I did this way before I concocted this plan – before I went to prison, in fact. I thought it was funny, because I knew the Magistrates would kill me, and I'd essentially be thanking them. But this is even funnier; indeed, a great joke to play on them.

So now I must change my will to include the name of the willing friend, once determined, and remove the business about actually killing me. Naturally, I can't mention the fact that it is payment for murder. I wouldn't want anyone doing Time on my account.

■■

This is, I now understand, the reason why I have returned to the written word after six years of silence. I've been waiting ten years for this to happen.

I knew this would happen. I've been waiting for this to happen. I've been waiting for ten years for this to happen. In truth, I've been waiting for this to happen. I've been waiting ten years for this to happen. I've been waiting. I've been waiting. I've been waiting for this to happen. I've been waiting ten years for this to happen. I've been waiting for this to happen. I've been waiting for this to happen for ten years. I've been waiting. For ten years, I've been waiting. For ten years, I've been waiting for this to happen. I've been waiting. I've been waiting. I've been waiting. I've been waiting for this to happen for ten years now. I've been waiting now for ten years for this to happen. I've been waiting. I've been waiting. I've been waiting.

Now.

Now, I'm still waiting.

Now, I will wait no longer.

■■

This is why this had to happen. So that I could know what it's like to be this character. You write everything before it happens – WHY? So that you can know, you know, because you always wanted to know. And now you know. So know that.

■■

I've settled upon the perfect man to kill me. He's one of my connections, so the idea of him being my killer appeals to me as the best of all possible solutions: first, because he is a close friend, because I like him and respect him and trust him, and believe that he is capable of much in this world – that if he wasn't pushing shit, he would be equally successful in some other field (should he have the opportunity [which I'd be providing], and should he choose to pursue another lifestyle [which he may not]); second, because I think it's brilliantly ironic: the man who sells me the shit that keeps me going, the shit that could kill me at one false shot, should indeed be my hired grim reaper. In a way, it doesn't seem like a big change in profession.

     I like it.

     I shall approach him soon.

■■

And he is that guy, too. There's a reason you came all this way. To here, to now. For *New Roses*. For *the Truth*, and for *the Flowers* to *Bloom*. Trust you. Believe me. This is where you can make that connection. What were you talking about and how can you talk about something without ever knowing the truth? Go fuck yourself. I am in pain. I know how painful it will be to get out of pain. Now you know. And soon you will know. Never.

■■

I called my friend and asked him to meet me at our regular spot, at the bar. We agreed upon the hour of midnight. I arrived early, as is my habit. I ordered a beer. New bartender – didn't recognize her. That's okay. I introduced myself. She was nice, she smiled. I got my beer and took it to the table in the far corner with the benches against both walls. It's my table. In this position, I can see everything; with my back to the wall, no one can get me without my seeing them first. I feel safe here, I can watch the people. It's also dark, and spatially suitable for illegal transactions.

     When I felt a change in the air I looked up to see my friend entering. Waiting for him to get a drink before joining me, I played the conversation over again in my mind, circulating the words I would use with him.

He sat down.

After I explained the situation, he stared at me. Neither aghast nor taken aback, but stoic, pensive, calm, so serious that his face betrayed a slight but noticeable perturbedness.

He continued unflinchingly looking at me. I waited silently: I had presented my case; the offer was on the table, and it was his turn to speak.

I waited.

Enough time passed that I finished the beer in front of me. I got up to get another – "You need one?" "Yeh," he managed without breaking his silence. When I returned, with two beers and two shots of whiskey, I noticed that his demeanor had changed – his body had loosened significantly. He was now leaning back in his chair, relaxed, lighter, freer.

I put the drinks on the table and smiled, turning and bending back down into my seat. I felt happy, truly happy. We raised our shots and clinked glasses.

"To your life, my friend," he spoke easily.

I smiled slowly, deeply, "Thank you," and we downed our shots.

"I almost said, 'Are you sure,' but figured that'd be a stupid question," he said. "You wouldn't have brought it up in the first place if you weren't sure. So I assume you've spent a lot of time thinking about this, right?"

"Of course," I replied. His confidence in me slightly surprised me, and filled me with great hope. At this moment, I felt closer to him than I've ever felt to anyone else. Perhaps he was the one person in the world who truly understood me. My tear ducts swelled slightly. I'm sure my eyes glazed over a bit. For the first time in a long time, I felt naturally happy. Life was good. I felt loved. I felt full of love. Everything was going to be all right, I knew this now, finally. Everything is going to be just fine, because I have achieved resolution.

"All right. When do you want this to happen?"

"On my birthday."

"This coming birthday? Like next week?"

I nodded. He shook his head reluctantly, as if it was too soon. I could see that it caused him great pain to agree to help me. I don't know how I'd become so close to him, over the past year, at this moment, why I felt so close to him, how I could feel so close to another person. It then occurred to me that I barely knew him at all.

I told him the time. I told him the place. I drew him a diagram of how it had been planned, illustrating the precise location on the block where I am to be taken and the exact points of insertion of the blade, so that when They would find my body, They would be certain that it was me who had, for the last Time, played them. All was set.

"Everything will be willed to you. You can trust me on that. Just make sure you destroy these drawings."

He nodded in understanding. "Of course."

We made plans for dinner that weekend. Over the past two years in the city, I actually have made a few friends. I know that I haven't mentioned them. As you know, I'm like that. I told him who I wanted to see there that night, and where I'd like for us to dine.

"It'll be my birthday dinner," I told him. "To, in fact, celebrate my life." He said he'd organize it for me. And with eyes that shone of regret he stated, cautiously, reluctantly, that he had to leave to meet up with somebody. "I understand, man. No worries." I smiled deeply, truly affected by it all.

"Speaking of which," he added, "you want something?"

I nodded, and he excused himself. When he returned from the bathroom, he sat down and passed me something under the table. "It's your usual order," he told me, (buy nine get one free), "and it's on the house."

I knew it would be futile to refuse the freebie and try to pay him. I accepted it with this knowledge.

We both rose from the table and gave each other a great hug. At that moment I could not help but to cry, and cry I did, and

I held him close, tightly, for what may have been a whole minute, sobbing. I breathed heavily, irregularly, difficultly, desperately, like a man saved from drowning, and he accepted me into him.

As he exited the bar, he looked back over his shoulder at me.

∎■■■∎

I stayed for another several drinks, thinking about everything. I thought about as much as I could.

I tried to put together the pieces of my life. I thought about everything I could remember about my life before my imprisonment. I thought about the time I spent inside, the time I spent at my old house after I got out, the past two years...

I was able only to place fragments of pieces of ideas of memories. Neverness. Where was I when I was there? I have always been wherever I was when I was there, though I have trouble believing this. I don't want to believe this. I want to believe that I never was. That I was never meant to be. No one deserves what I've had to deal with: constant persecution by the Ones I was born to serve.

I wanted to.
I wanted to.
I wanted to.
But I couldn't.
I just couldn't.
I don't think I was allowed.

At this point I came to ask myself: Is it me, or is it Them? Because I can accept that, that Truth, if the Truth means that it is Them. Then everything can be explained away, and I can rest at peace, knowing that I performed my duties according to my station during my time allotted here on this here place here.

Who was I then, who was I before then, who was I when I am was, who is I now, who are I be when I am not be? These are questions that, no matter how much they may interest me at this point, no longer bear any relevance to my life, to my story, to what constitutes my *New Roses*.

For I accept that I have now reached the end. I have accepted my end. This is my role – I know for a fact that this is my role.

It is a unique moment, indeed a once-in-a-lifetime experience, to accept one's part in one's own Death. I am simultaneously complicit and noncompliant. I have denied, escaped, welcomed, accepted, refuted, foiled, planned, staged, and commissioned my own Death. With their wishes, against their wishes. If I have produced One Work of Art during my lifetime, it will be this. This, and only this.

In the end, having remained in the bar for hours, thinking, nothing of any real value occurred to me – just a wrecked and meaningless comfortable platitude of thereness. None of it, meaning my life, seemed important. I felt a great ease come over me, a liberating release, a newfound lightness of being. I sat at my table and worked leisurely at my drinks, comfortably calm and content and meaningless. I breathed slowly, deeply, easily, quietly.

The only feeling I can describe having at that moment is one of timelessness; as if I was finally there, in the here, as if I had finally arrived at where I had always been meant to be, finally, anxious neither of the past nor the future – for I was in control of my future, now –, a feeling of being one with the present, my being feeling the collapse of space to make way for its fusion with Time.

For the first time in my life, I was in the here and now.

I closed the bar. When the bartender kindly informed me, well after four, that it was time to get going, I felt remarkably clear-minded and aware, comfortable and at peace.

I rose to my feet, thanked her kindly, and left the bar.

Emerging out onto the street, I saw that the night was transforming into a pleasant winter pre-dawn. The sun would begin its ascent within the hour. I looked up at the dark purple-gray starless sky and decided, instead of taking the subway or a taxi, to walk the thirty minutes or so home to my apartment. I wanted to be outside, to feel the cold air against my skin, to witness the first breaths of a new day, to smell and hear and move and enter and become and exist as part of the new city morning, part of the environment alive about me.

I turned up the street, with comfort and ease of purpose, and started walking homeward.

A cool breeze played softly with my face and stirred the last of the remaining leaves of the occasional trees that lined the streets. A slight drizzle began to fall, calmly descending upon the city and upon my skin like a thin cloud of soft wet pine needles. It felt good to be a little cold, a little wet.

As the streets gathered more of the rain, the lights of the city night began to play their tricks upon the pavement and the sidewalk beneath my feet. I could see the traffic lights casually changing from red to green and from green to yellow to red as reflections upon the slick surface of the ground and across the glass windows of the storefronts and the buildings that lined the streets. There was a near-audible silence in the air that only occurs on weekday mornings in certain areas of the city on off-garbage days between the short window of time just after the night people have made it home from the bars and just before the early risers open their doors to take their dogs out before heading to work to beat the morning rush. Or so I gathered.

I was neither drunk nor sober, and I embraced the sublime ease of not being in a hurry – of leaving nothing and heading nowhere. Of a new freedom. My new freedom. I had actually achieved it. I was done. I attained resolution; my time was defined.

A general warmth filled me, despite the coolness of the night. I felt good. The world around me seemed to be all in accord. The sacred stillness of the city captivated me, captured me, and held me close, anticipating nowness, carrying me along my timeless stroll. I found my feet leading me towards the river, where I arrived upon a lone park bench. I sat down upon the damp wood and waited there, motionless, sitting there, waiting for the sun to lift up a new day.

And when the large, round, orange star appeared in all of its full glory, scattering its light haphazardly across the ripples of the water, shining upon my naked face and illuminating the facades of the first row of buildings that line the river, I rose to my feet and continued my journey home.

I made it to my apartment without having noted a single passer-by. I made it up the stairs, entered my room, laid down on my bed, and went to sleep.

AFTERWARDS, AN INTRODUCTION.

When I first finally read *New Roses* in October, 2007, I immediately arranged for its publication, courtesy of the Body without Organs (BwO). It was the least i could do.
      Years later, this Whisk(e)y Tit Books edition is a great honor to the memory of its author. The Organization asked me to write something for it, and this is it.

(things that i know).

New Roses is a work of fiction.
      Regarding possible autobiographical actualities in the text, I know that he did not write the following parts:

        -*A Note from the Editors*.
        -Medical examiner's report.
        -List of personal possessions.

      The rest of the book is real.

∎ ■

The first section of *New Roses*, "the truth," originated in 1997, and has existed in many forms.

The second section, "the garden," is the result of the application of Reductionism on "the truth." Reductionism is an experiment in reprocessing a text by the omission of all subsequent occurrences of a word following its initial instantiation. In this specific case, the author tracked every word that appears in "the truth" and deleted every recurrence of every word. Stripping the text of lexical repetition produced the story-teller's elemental vocabulary, revealing the very foundation of his absolute reality.

In terms of the story, years pass between the end of "the truth" and the beginning of "the flowers bloom." During his years of incarceration, the author lost the ability to communicate with words. Therefore, "the garden" serves as a symbol of the passage of time; it is a physical placeholder. Which is why it doesn't necessarily matter if you read "the garden" carefully or if you skim through it: the simple act of flipping through the pages takes time, and thereby functions as a representation of the years that language failed him, or evaded him.

I am grateful for the opportunity to have worked on this project. Thank you for reading.

With Respect,

Stefan O. Rak
(nearly all of 2019)

"I began writing with no precise goal, animated chiefly by a desire to forget, at least for the time being, the things I can be or do personally. Thus, at first, I thought that the character speaking in the first person had no relation to me."

-Georges Bataille
"Part 2. Coincidences"
Story of the Eye

Published in the United States by Whisk(e)y Tit: www.whiskeytit.com. If you wish to use or reproduce all or part of this book for any means, please let the author and publisher know. You're pretty much required to, legally.

ISBN 978-1-7329596-8-2

First Whisk(e)y Tit paperback edition. Previously published by the author.

www.ingramcontent.com/pod-product-compliance
Lightning Source LLC
Chambersburg PA
CBHW071528110726
47908CB00003B/984